LOVING
LIBBY

Also by Robin Lee Hatcher

Coming to America Series

Dear Lady

Patterns of Love

In His Arms

Promised to Me

LOVING LIBBY

ROBIN LEE HATCHER

Formerly titled *Liberty Blue*

ZONDERVAN

ZONDERVAN.com/
AUTHORTRACKER
follow your favorite authors

Loving Libby
Copyright © 1995, 2005 by Robin Lee Hatcher
Previously published as *Liberty Blue* by HarperCollins *Publishers*

Value Edition, 978-0-310-29225-8

Requests for information should be addressed to:

Zondervan, *Grand Rapids, Michigan* 49530

Library of Congress Cataloging-in-Publication Data

Hatcher, Robin Lee.
     Loving Libby / Robin Lee Hatcher.
        p. cm.
     Originally published as Liberty Blue. New York: Harper, 1995. (revised content)
     ISBN 978-0-310-25690-8
     I. Title.
  PS3558.A73574 L68 2005
  813'.54—dc22

                                     2005010117

Interior design by Michelle Espinoza

Printed in the United States of America

---

08 09 10 11 12 13 14 15 • 19 18 17 16 15 14 13 12 11 10 9 8 7 6 5 4 3 2 1

To those who understand the joy of second chances.
And to the Lord who covers us with His grace,
removing our sins, as far from us
as the east is from the west.

Stone walls do not a prison make,
Nor iron bars a cage;
Minds innocent and quiet take
That for an hermitage;
If I have freedom in my love,
And in my soul am free,
Angels alone that soar above
Enjoy such liberty.

Richard Lovelace

I run in the path of your commands,
for you have set my heart free.

Psalm 119:32 NIV

One

May 1890
Blue Springs Ranch, Idaho Territory

"Not again, Bevins," Libby whispered to herself as she peered at the horseman's approach through the latticework of sunlight and shadows. "Not as long as I've got breath in my body."

Obscured by the thick grove of cottonwoods and pines, the rider stopped his horse. Libby had difficulty keeping track of him as dusk settled over the barnyard. Whatever he was up to, it wasn't good. It never was with Timothy Bevins.

She stepped back from the window until certain she couldn't be seen, then moved to the front door, checking to see if it was tightly latched. It was.

A small sigh of relief escaped her. But her relief was short-lived. Bevins wouldn't break into her house. No, that method was too direct and could get him in trouble with the law. He would take an underhanded approach.

Well, you can't scare me off.

She pressed her lips into a determined line. She wasn't going anywhere, frightened or not. And she wouldn't wait for Bevins to make the first move either. She wouldn't give him a chance to do his dirty work. Not this time.

She grabbed the double-barreled shotgun that rested against the wall. Then, fortifying herself with a deep breath, she walked to Sawyer's bedroom, peeking inside at the boy lying on the bed.

"Sawyer, something's got the horses worked up. Probably another coyote. I'm going out to run it off. If you hear anything, don't be scared. It's just me."

"I don't scare so easy, Libby." He raised his scabbed-over chin to a brave tilt.

"I know you don't." *And neither do I.*

She hurried through the kitchen to the back door, opened it silently, and stepped outside. Evening had changed the colors of the earth and sky into varying shades of gray and black. The trees were threatening silhouettes, looming overhead, their scraggly arms reaching toward her.

Bevins could be anywhere. Perhaps he watched her even now.

She sidled along the side of the house, making her way toward the wide clearing at the front, searching every shadow.

You can't scare me, you yellow-bellied snake in the grass. You can't run me off my land.

Libby quit running over six years ago. This was her home, her land. Aunt Amanda had entrusted the ranch to Libby, and she meant to protect it and everyone on it. She wouldn't let Timothy Bevins run her off, no matter what he did, no matter what he threatened to do. And he wouldn't get another chance to hurt Sawyer either. Spooking the boy's horse was the last straw. Absolutely the last straw.

She heard the snap of a twig off to her right. Startled, she turned and, in the waning light, saw him stepping out of the trees. More important, she saw the rifle in his hand.

She reacted instinctively, raising the shotgun and firing before he had a chance to do the same. The kick of the gun slammed her back against the side of the house as she squeezed off the second shot.

She gasped for air, her ears ringing, her shoulder throbbing. Had either shot hit Bevins? She hoped not. She only meant to scare him. As her vision cleared, she looked across the yard and saw him lying in the dirt.

He didn't move.

Oh, Lord. Don't let him be dead. Don't let me be guilty of murder.

Gulping down panic, she dropped the shotgun and cautiously made her way toward him, uncertain what she would do if he was dead, uncertain what she should do if he wasn't.

She reminded herself that Bevins was to blame for the death of Dan Deevers, Sawyer's father. Dan, her ranch foreman, had been out in that January ice storm because Bevins ran off more of her sheep. He'd been stealing them a few at a time for the past year. She knew it was him, but she couldn't prove it. Just like she couldn't prove he'd spooked Sawyer's horse on purpose yesterday. The boy could have broken his neck in that fall.

The Good Book said not to hate a man, but Libby had a problem with that command when it came to Bevins.

Reaching him, she steeled herself against a bloody sight, then looked down.

Father God, what have I done?

Libby dropped to her knees and stared at the man she'd shot. It wasn't Bevins. It wasn't one of Bevins's hired thugs. It was someone she'd never seen before.

God forgive her. She'd killed an innocent man.

The stranger groaned.

With a quick prayer of thanks that he wasn't dead after all, Libby sprang into action. She had to stanch the bleeding. No time to wonder who he was or what he'd been doing, sneaking around her place at this time of evening.

She raced to the house, wishing for once that she hadn't forsaken her long skirts and petticoats for the freedom of denim britches. Cotton petticoats made good bandages.

As soon as she opened the door, she saw Sawyer, bracing himself against the jamb of his bedroom.

"What happened, Libby? What's out there?"

A heartbeat's hesitation, then she hurried forward. She couldn't stop and explain. "Go back to bed, Sawyer."

"Libby —"

"Now!"

Before Sawyer turned away, Libby caught a glimpse of tears in his eyes, but she knew better than to apologize. Sawyer was every bit as proud as his father had been and wouldn't want her to see him crying.

She grabbed a blanket off her bed. It was almost dark and the temperature was dropping. She had to get the stranger inside. In another few minutes, it would be black as pitch out there, not to mention bone-chilling cold.

Her heart pounding, Libby returned to the wounded man. She laid the blanket on the earth beside him, then paused to assess the situation. The long and lanky stranger had a good sixty pounds on her, if not more. But Libby was strong. She wrestled enough obstinate sheep at the Blue Springs Ranch to make her so. She ought to be able to handle one helpless male.

Bending over, ignoring the crimson stains on his pant leg and shirt, she rolled him onto the blanket. She grabbed hold of one end and began to drag the injured man across the yard, making slow but steady progress. Worry nagged the edges of her conscience.

What would the sheriff do to her if the stranger died? Would anyone believe she'd fired in self-defense? What was the penalty for shooting someone in cold blood? Hanging? Prison?

She shook off such thoughts. Only a fool or a thief — or both — would have done what this man did. No honest traveler would hide in the trees rather than ride into the yard and knock on her door. No, this was the stranger's own fault.

She wished Alistair McGregor or Ronald Aberdeen were here to help her. They would know what to do. But they were with the sheep, up in the hills north of the ranch.

Just as well. As fond as she was of McGregor, Libby wasn't in the mood for a lecture from the crusty Scotsman.

She dragged the unconscious man into Amanda's old bedroom. Once there, she turned up the lamp and set it on the floor where it could spill the most light onto the stranger's wounds. She felt her stomach turn.

Buck up, Libby. You've got no business getting squeamish at the first sight of blood.

She'd seen worse than this. She might see worse yet before the year was out. Life in the Idaho high country was hard. It always had been. It always would be.

With her sewing shears, she cut open his shirt and trousers, swallowing hard as she stared at the torn and bleeding flesh on his left side and leg. There wasn't time for misplaced modesty. City girls could blush and swoon, but Libby would be sensible.

Her gaze moved from his wounds to his face. He didn't look like a thief. Come to think of it, he didn't look like a fool either. And he certainly looked nothing like Timothy Bevins.

The stranger's features were aristocratic without any hint of softness. His nose was long and straight, his jaw strong and determined. A slight cleft dented his square chin. Black brows capped eyes that bore tiny crow's-feet in the outer corners. A two-day-old beard made other men look scraggly and unkempt, but not this man.

He groaned again.

Libby rose from the floor and hurried to the kitchen, where she poured hot water into a large bowl. She dropped a towel into the basin, then picked up the soap and returned to the bedroom.

"Mister," she muttered, "I sure hope you don't come to, because this is going to hurt."

Pain was Remington's constant companion. He dwelled in darkness, haunted by blurry visions and hot pokers jabbing into his flesh.

He saw his father once, far in the distance. He wanted to go to him, but he couldn't move. He tried to call to him, but he couldn't speak. Slowly his father faded, swallowed in a white mist, leaving Remington alone with the pain once more.

No. Don't go.
But his father was gone.

"No ... don't go ..."

Libby leaned over the man in the bed, uncertain whether she'd heard him. "Mister?"

His eyes were closed, his face drawn with pain, as it had been for two days. The wound in his side seemed superficial, but Libby was concerned about his leg. The buckshot had torn through it, missing the bone but tearing the flesh and muscle. She wondered if he'd ever walk without a limp. And there was the possibility of infection. So many things could go wrong before he had a chance to recover.

With a shake of her head, Libby straightened, picked up the washbasin, and carried it outside to empty into the underbrush. Overhead, the sky was an expanse of brilliant blue, unmarred by clouds. The air was warm and would have seemed hot if not for the breeze.

She sighed as she pushed stray wisps of hair from her face, wondering what she would do about the stranger if he didn't show signs of improvement soon. McGregor wouldn't come down from Tyler Creek, where the sheep grazed, for several weeks. Not until she failed to show up on time with fresh supplies. It was a two-day ride to find the nearest doctor. She couldn't send Sawyer for the physician, couldn't leave the patient in a ten-year-old boy's care while she went, and couldn't haul a seriously wounded man all that distance in the wagon. It seemed she had no choice but to wait it out, doin the best doctoring she could on her own.

Turning, she noticed Sawyer looking at the man's horse in the corral. She set the empty washbasin near the back door and crossed the yard to stand beside him.

"He's a mighty nice horse, ain't he, Libby?"

"Isn't. Not ain't," she corrected gently. "Yes, he's a fine horse."

Fine was an understatement. The bay gelding was magnificent. This was no ten-dollar saddle horse. This was a steed more commonly found in a stable behind a New York mansion on Fifth Avenue or at a summer cottage in Newport. Not the usual sort of horseflesh seen in these parts. But neither was the gelding's owner the usual sort of man to show up at her ranch. Most men who came this way were itinerant workers, traveling around the country, looking for anything to put a few dollars in their pockets before moving on. No, the man lying in Amanda's bed was no more like them than his horse was like Idaho's mountain mustangs.

She thought of the beautiful saddle she'd removed from the gelding's back, the fancy leather saddlebags, the expensive cut of the stranger's clothes, the gold pocket watch, the Colt revolvers, the Winchester rifle. She recalled every item that belonged to him, including the money she'd found. But nothing gave up his identity. He remained a mystery — as did the reason for his arrival at Blue Springs.

"Is he gonna be all right, Libby?"

She glanced at the boy. Sawyer's coffee-colored hair was shaggy and sorely in need of a trim. His eyes, like dark brown saucers, watched her with a wariness she understood. Nothing was certain out here. Life was precarious. Sawyer had learned this sooner than most.

"I'm pretty sure he'll make it." She brushed his tousled hair from his forehead.

He frowned and withdrew. Sawyer wanted her to treat him like a man, not a baby. He often told her so.

Libby's heart tightened in her chest. She loved Sawyer, and she wanted to do right by him. But what did she know about raising children? She certainly couldn't take anything from her own childhood as an example.

For a moment, she recalled paper-covered walls, high ceilings and elaborate moldings, long hallways and whispering servants, a mother with a sad-sweet smile, a father who —

She beat the memories back.

Libby looked at Sawyer again. "You'd better feed the horses, then get inside and prop that ankle up before the swelling returns."

"It don't hurt no more."

"It *doesn't* hurt *any*more."

"Right." He tossed the word over his shoulder as he headed toward the barn.

She smiled to herself. Sawyer could probably run a footrace and not bother his ankle. She shouldn't make an invalid out of him.

If only the patient inside the house would mend as quickly. She had a nagging feeling his presence didn't bode well for her future. She would be glad to see him out of that bed in the spare room and on his way.

Remington drifted slowly into consciousness. At first he thought he only dreamed of the pain. How wrong he was.

What happened?

He searched his memory for clues. He remembered arriving in Idaho. He remembered talking to folks in Boise City and Weiser. He remembered learning about, then looking for, the Blue Springs Ranch.

The ranch. That was it. He'd found it at dusk. He'd dismounted and left his horse in the trees, then started to walk toward the house.

And then what?

A noise.

A gunshot.

And then pain. White-hot pain.

With his eyes still closed, he moved his right hand to check his injuries. He felt the strips of bandages binding his chest and winced when he touched a tender place on his left side.

He continued his exploration, moving his hand beneath the blanket toward the throbbing in his left thigh. How serious was it?

He drew a ragged breath, then opened his eyes, squinting against the sunlight that streamed through the open window into an unfamiliar room. He tried to lift his head from the pillow but sank back as agony exploded behind his eyes.

A moment later, he lost consciousness again.

Two

SENSING ANOTHER'S PRESENCE THE NEXT time he awakened, Remington lay still, eyes closed, listening and waiting, not ready to let anyone know he was conscious. Even so, he flinched when fingers touched his leg and slowly began to remove the dressing on his wound.

"Sorry, mister." The woman's soft, warm voice prompted him to open his eyes far enough to glimpse his nurse. Her rose-gold hair fell over one shoulder in a thick braid. She wore an apple-green shirt, a perfect match with the color of her eyes. Her cheeks and the bridge of her pert nose were freckled from too much time in the sun.

Little about her resembled the young lady in the portrait he'd seen hanging above the fireplace in the drawing room at Rosegate; little matched the detailed description Anna Vanderhoff had given him. Yet he knew without a shred of doubt he was looking at Anna's daughter, Olivia — and a bonus of two hundred fifty thousand dollars.

"Libby?"

Remington closed his eyes.

"Libby, I don't think the runt's gettin' enough to eat. The other pups keep pushin' him out."

Did Olivia have a child? No, the boy had called her Libby, not Mother. Besides, the kid sounded too old to be hers. Was the boy a stepchild? Could there be a husband in the picture?

"I think we oughta bring him in the house and feed him ourselves," the boy continued. "He oughta be able to suck on one of them bottles, like an orphaned lamb."

"You know how Aunt Amanda felt about dogs in the house."

He liked her voice. It had a whiskey-coated quality and a hint of a western twang. But Olivia Vanderhoff was not from the West. She was born and raised in Manhattan, summering at the Vanderhoff seaside estate in Rhode Island, and was schooled at the finest women's academy that money and privilege could buy.

"But Miz Blue's gone, Libby. It's up to you now."

Remington heard her sigh.

"Yes, it is up to me, Sawyer." She was silent a moment. "I'll tell you what. I'll come have a look at that pup as soon as I'm finished here."

"How's he doin'?"

Remington sensed Olivia looking at him during the pause that followed.

"As well as can be expected. But I wish he'd wake up. He needs nourishment."

"He's gonna be okay, Libby. You'll see. God'll take care of him."

"I hope so," she whispered. "I truly hope so."

Remington hoped so too. He needed to send a telegram to New York City.

Libby worked with deliberate care as she cleansed the stranger's wounds, then replaced the soiled bandages. When she finished, she picked up the basin of water and blood-stained strips of linen and rose from the chair beside the bed. Only then did she allow her gaze to return to the man's face.

Lord, let Sawyer be right. Let this man be okay. Let him wake up soon.

It was her fault he was lying there, unconscious and in pain. It was her fault he was wounded, perhaps crippled for life. How would she ever make it up to him — *if* he survived?

Another thought plagued her. Did he have a wife, a worried wife who waited to hear from him?

Unable to stop herself, Libby reached forward and brushed his black hair away from his forehead. The moment her fingertips touched him, unease coiled in her stomach. She pulled back her hand and hurried from the room.

Father God, heal him and take him away. I feel like we're in danger as long as he's here. Is that Your Spirit or my lack of faith?

Libby carried the bowl of water to the kitchen and set it on the counter. She dropped the soiled bandages into a basket, then went out to the barn as she'd promised. She found Sawyer in a far corner, kneeling in the straw. He held the black-and-white runt of the litter in his arms. Misty, the puppy's mother, lifted her head as Libby approached. The dog's big, round eyes begged for relief from the eight rambunctious pups latched onto her belly.

Libby knelt beside Sawyer and stroked Misty's head. "Poor girl," she crooned. "Can't wait until they're weaned, can you?"

Misty licked her hand.

Libby pulled two of the plump three-week-old pups away from their breakfast, setting them behind her in the thick straw. Then she took the runt from Sawyer's hands and pressed the pup's nose against Misty's belly, holding him there until he grabbed hold. "Sawyer, let's try helping him out this way for a while. It'll be better for him if he gets his food from his mother."

"Okay." His voice revealed disappointment.

She was tempted to tell him he could bring the puppy into the house, but old habits die hard. She could hear Amanda's voice in her head: "*These dogs work for their keep. They ain't pets. They're here to tend the flock and send up an alarm if there's trouble, and for no other reasons than that. Don't you go makin' pets of 'em, Libby. You hear me?*"

She smiled at the memory. Against Amanda's orders, Misty became Libby's pet. But Amanda hadn't really minded. She understood Libby's loneliness, a loneliness the collie helped to fill.

Libby glanced at Sawyer, her smile fading. The boy was lonely too. He missed his father. Libby understood. She knew all about missing someone until a body thought it might die from the missing. She'd felt that way about her mother. She still did sometimes, even all these years later.

"You're kind of partial to that runt, aren't you?" She wanted to put her arm around Sawyer, wanted to show him she loved him.

He shrugged.

"How about if we make the pup yours?"

The boy's brown eyes widened as he looked up at her.

"It'll be your job to train him, see that he learns to earn his keep. Can you do that?"

Sawyer nodded, and his shaggy hair fell into his eyes.

"All right, then. He's yours."

She thought for a moment he might hug her, but he caught himself in time.

"Thanks, Libby. I'll make him a good sheepdog. I promise. We'll take care of the sheep for you. You'll see."

"I know you will." *It's okay to be a little boy, Sawyer. You don't have to take your father's place.* She rose from the barn floor. "Don't forget you've got other chores to do."

"I won't." His gaze remained locked on his puppy.

Libby headed for the barn door, thinking it likely she would find Sawyer right where she left him come lunchtime. As she stepped through the opening, she squinted her eyes against the bright midmorning sunlight. It was going to be another hot day.

"Mornin', Miss Blue."

She stopped short, and her breath caught in her chest.

Timothy Bevins sat astride his horse, his mouth curving in a mockery of a smile. Some women might have found him appealing, but Libby saw only the smallness of his soul behind his hazel eyes. Amanda had said he was a coward without enough gumption to stand up for himself unless he knew for certain he was stronger than his victim.

"What are you doing here, Mr. Bevins?"

He leaned his forearms on the pommel of his saddle, his body relaxed yet somehow threatening. "Now, that don't sound neighborly. I come by to see how you're doin'. I'm worried about you bein' here all alone, now that your foreman's dead and old McGregor's gone with the sheep."

She held herself straight. "You needn't be worried about me. I can take care of myself."

"This ain't friendly country. You know that, Miss Blue. Just about anything can happen." He dismounted and took one step toward her.

Bevins wasn't a tall man, perhaps three or four inches taller than Libby, but he was all muscle, his body sculpted by years of working the range. It wouldn't take much for him to overpower her.

Libby glanced toward the house, longing for the shotgun that rested against the wall inside the doorway. She was angered by the threat she perceived in his words, in his actions. He had no right to come on her ranch and make her feel helpless.

Bevins moved into her line of vision. "Have you given more thought to sellin'? You don't belong on a place like this, Miss Blue. You should get yourself a man t'care for you. Think how much happier you'd be. It'd be better for that boy too." He shook his head. "Anything could happen to him out here. Why, he could get hurt real bad just any old time."

Libby forgot her uneasiness. She forgot the shotgun in the house. She stepped forward, her head held high, her hands balled into fists at her sides. "Get off my land. And don't you try to hurt Sawyer again."

"Now, Miss Blue" — he smiled a smile that made her stiffen with fury — "don't go gettin' yourself in a tizzy. I'm just sayin' — "

"I know what you're saying, Mr. Bevins. And I'm saying, *Get off my land.*"

He grabbed her by the arms. His smile vanished. "I do believe you need someone to show you your place."

"Let go of me." She tried to pull free, but his grip only tightened.

"Maybe I'm just the man to show you."

She was too angry to be afraid. "Let go of me." She tried again to pull free.

Instead of letting go, he yanked her closer. She smelled his hot, unpleasant breath on her face.

Realizing her vulnerability at last, fear replaced rage, turning her mouth dry and her knees to water. "Let go of me," she whispered.

Bevins laughed, low and ugly.

"The lady said to let her go."

Libby gasped, and Bevins took a half step back, although his grip remained firm. In unison, they looked toward the house. There, standing outside the door, leveling a rifle at Bevins, was the stranger she'd left unconscious not fifteen minutes ago. He wore the trousers Libby had mended and patched, but his chest and feet were bare. Despite that, he looked surprisingly capable of taking on Bevins.

"Who're you?" Bevins demanded.

"That's none of your business. Now, let the lady go."

Bevins's hold on her arms loosened, and she pulled away, stepping out of his reach, surprised that her legs held her upright.

The man motioned with his Winchester. "Get on your horse and ride out."

Bevins glared at him, then at Libby.

"Now."

Bevins apparently believed the warning sincere. He swung onto his horse's back and kicked the roan into a canter, riding into the thick grove of trees.

Libby stared after him. It took an effort to breathe, and her legs were still shaking. If not for the stranger, Bevins might have done more than frighten her. She turned to look at her rescuer again just as his Winchester clattered to the earth. She saw him grab for the doorjamb, miss it, then slump down beside the rifle.

Libby rushed across the barnyard. As she knelt on the ground, she noticed a red stain darkening the leg of his trousers. He opened his eyes. Blue eyes, the color of the Idaho sky before a thunderstorm blew through.

"Is he gone?" he asked.

"Yes."

"Good." The word came out on a sigh as his eyes drifted closed.

Six hours later, he regained consciousness.

Relief flooded Libby. "Hello. I'm glad to see you're back."

His eyes focused on her face, but he didn't speak.

"Thank you for what you did."

"How long have I been unconscious?" His brows drew together in a frown of concentration.

"Since this morning. About six hours."

"No. How long since I was shot?"

"Five days."

He closed his eyes. "How bad is my leg?"

She hesitated. "I think it will be all right." She sank onto the chair near the bed, her guilt returning. "There doesn't seem to be any infection. Of course, it would have been better if you hadn't walked on it" — he opened his eyes again, his disconcerting gaze locking with hers — "but I'm very glad you did."

"He was disturbing my sleep."

She ignored his weak attempt at humor. "I'm in your debt, sir, especially since I'm the one who . . . especially after I . . ." She let her words drift away, uncertain how to continue.

His blue gaze studied her for a long time before he said, "I take it you had something to do with my injuries."

Her mind replayed the moment she'd shot him. She could so easily have killed him.

"Why'd you shoot me?"

"I thought you were Bevins." She tilted her head toward the window. "The man who was here today."

He released a sigh. "I guess I can understand then." He winced. "I'd have shot too if I were you."

This time, his wry tone made her smile.

Remington had thoroughly studied the portrait of Olivia Vanderhoff during his visit to Rosegate, the Vanderhoffs' Seventy-second Street mansion in Manhattan, but clearly the artist failed to capture the real essence of his subject. The girl in the portrait had no sparkle in her green eyes, nor promise of laughter around her pretty mouth. At seventeen, she'd posed for the portrait in a gown of white lace and satin, her hair dressed with pearls, her throat accented with a gold locket. Now she was twenty-five, clad in a man's shirt and trousers. She wore no pearls, no locket, no jewelry of any kind.

What made you choose this stark life, Miss Vanderhoff? Why this?

But the why wasn't of any real importance. The only thing that mattered was he'd found Northrop Vanderhoff's missing daughter. With the money he would collect for locating the beautiful heiress, Remington might be able to keep his promise to avenge his father's death.

He saw a flush of pink steal into her cheeks and realized he was staring. All traces of her smile and suppressed laughter vanished. She straightened her back, lifted her chin, and held out her hand toward him.

"Introductions are past due, sir. My name is Libby Blue. I'm the owner of the Blue Springs Ranch."

He took hold of her hand. "It's a pleasure to meet you, Mrs. Blue. My name's Remington Walker."

"It's *Miss* Blue."

So there wasn't a husband after all. That was good news.

"What brought you to my ranch, Mr. Walker?"

Only a very few folks had ever fooled Remington. Libby Blue, as she called herself, wasn't going to be one of them. He called upon his ability to read people and saw intelligence in her eyes, as well as a healthy dose of caution and a dash of distrust. He also sensed an innate honesty.

Fortunately Remington wasn't troubled by his conscience when it came to fabricating identities or histories for himself. When tracking down fugitives, one was required to do or say many things an otherwise honest person wouldn't do or say. He'd been hired to take Olivia Vanderhoff back to New York, and if that meant earning her trust through lies, so be it.

He feigned a self-deprecating chuckle. "I thought it was sheer luck that I stumbled onto this place, until you shot me."

The blush in her cheeks deepened, but her gaze didn't waver.

"I was lost, Miss Blue. I was in the territorial capital on business and decided I'd have a look at the country before returning to my home. I had a map and thought I could head off into the wilderness, explore a bit of the territory, then find my way back, none the worse for wear. As you've no doubt guessed, I lost my way. But then I came across your place."

"Why didn't you ride up in the open where you could be seen?" Her eyes narrowed. "Why'd you leave your horse in the trees and come to the house carrying a rifle?"

"Bad judgment on my part."

He could tell she weighed his words carefully. Then the suspicion left her gaze, and a hint of her pretty smile touched the corners of her mouth again.

"You're not from around here, Mr. Walker. I can tell by your accent. Where are you from?"

"I was born and raised in Virginia, ma'am." Like the name he'd given, that was the truth.

"Well, I suggest you return there as soon as you're able to travel." She rose from the chair, her expression stern but her tone teasing. "We do things a bit differently here in Idaho."

"Shoot first?" Remington rested the palm of his right hand on his left side. "I noticed." Then he grinned to take the sting out of his words.

Libby's pulse quickened. Alarmed by her reaction to his smile, she stepped toward the door. "You must be hungry. There's a kettle of stew on the stove. I'll bring you some broth. You need food in your stomach." She hurried out of the bedroom.

Never trust a stranger. Never. I know better. Don't trust him, no matter what.

Keeping her guard up was a rule that had served her well for over six years. It was a rule she couldn't afford to abandon — not even for this particular stranger's devastating smile.

Unbidden, unwanted, the memory of her father intruded. A regal man with steel-gray hair and eyes to match. A man who bought and sold people the same way he bought and sold property or ships or anything else. A man for whom everything and everyone had a price. Even his daughter. She was to have brought him the southern railroad he coveted for so many years.

Libby closed her eyes as she leaned against the sideboard. She didn't want to think about her father. To do so only made her unhappy. She couldn't change who he was or how little she'd meant to him.

Her mother's image drifted into her thoughts, and Libby felt the sting of tears. "Oh, Mama," she whispered, her heart aching.

She wondered if her mother knew she was all right. Dan Deevers had mailed Libby's letter from Cheyenne when he was there last year, but she couldn't know if Anna Vanderhoff received it. It had been a foolish thing to do, writing to her mother after years of careful silence. But Amanda Blue's death brought loneliness, and Libby missed her mother with a keen freshness.

Libby sniffed and opened her eyes. She was being melodramatic. The Lord had given her a good life here at the Blue

Springs. She owned her land and her sheep and her home. She had Sawyer to love, and she had McGregor and young Ronald, trusted friends. Nobody owned her. She wasn't trapped in a loveless marriage to a godless man.

Drawing a deep breath, she filled a bowl with broth, placed it on a tray, and carried it back to the bedroom. She needed to get Mr. Walker well and on his way — and the sooner the better.

Three

IF REMINGTON DIDN'T KNOW BETTER, he would have thought Libby had spent her entire life doctoring men in the back-country instead of hobnobbing with the sons and daughters of New York's Knickerbocker families. Still, he was glad to take over tending his own wounds after one week of her excellent care. It didn't seem right, having her do it. Not when he knew what he intended.

Remington's injuries would take time to heal, and even though he couldn't afford to lose that time, neither did he relish the prospect of walking with a limp the rest of his days. He suspected that might happen if he tried to leave the ranch too soon.

He clenched his teeth as he cleansed the wound on his thigh. Stabs of pain shot up and down his leg. To distract himself, Remington thought about Libby. He had memorized the tiny wisps that curled at her temples, the unusual color of her pale rose-gold hair, her tiny shell-shaped ears, the small point of her chin. He recalled the sweep of her thick eyelashes, the delicate arch of her golden brows, and the smoothness of her skin. He decided he even liked the splash of freckles over her nose.

What made you run, Libby Blue? Why did you leave a life of ease for this?

He thought of Northrop Vanderhoff, standing behind his large cherrywood desk, a glass of brandy in his hand, his thick gray eyebrows drawn together as he had glared at Remington.

"I hear you're the best, Walker."

"If she can be found, I'll find her," Remington had answered, his gaze never wavering, his expression hiding the bitterness that seethed in his chest. It galled him that Northrop either didn't know Remington was Jefferson Walker's son or didn't care. Or perhaps Northrop had forgotten Remington's father altogether. After so many years, why should he remember a man he'd helped ruin? Jefferson Walker hadn't been the first nor the last casualty of Northrop Vanderhoff's greed.

Well, Northrop might forget, but Remington never would. Never. Not until he evened the score.

"I want my daughter returned to me," Northrop had continued. "I'll make it well worth your time. You find her and bring her back."

At first Remington suspected Olivia Vanderhoff ran off with a man her father didn't approve of. It wasn't unheard of for girls of good breeding to do that. But his investigation hadn't turned up a mystery lover.

So what made you run, Olivia, if it wasn't love?

Half an hour later, when Libby came to collect the soiled bandages and washbasin, Remington decided to seek the answer to his question. "Has this ranch always been your home, Miss Blue?"

A strange expression flickered in her eyes as she lifted her gaze to meet his. "I came to live with Aunt Amanda over six years ago."

Remington knew she had no aunt, living here or anywhere else. "And before that, where did you live?"

"San Francisco."

That much was true. San Francisco was where he'd picked up her trail.

Libby dropped the bandages into the basin that she held in the crook of her arm. "I'll bring you something to eat. Porridge might sit well on your stomach."

He made a face. He hated oatmeal.

She laughed, a light, airy sound that filled the room.

"Mr. Walker, you and Sawyer have something in common. He doesn't think much of my porridge either. But Aunt Amanda said it was good food for the sickbed, and she was seldom wrong. So I'll fix it, and you'll eat it."

"Yes, ma'am."

Still smiling, Libby left the room.

Remington grinned too. At least he wouldn't be bored during his convalescence. Discovering how Olivia Vanderhoff had transformed herself into Libby Blue would prove an interesting diversion until he could finish the job he'd come here to do.

Sawyer waited until Libby was hanging clothes on the line before he ventured over to the bedroom door and peered inside.

When Mr. Walker saw him in the doorway, he said, "You must be Sawyer."

He nodded.

"Come on in."

Sawyer glanced toward the back door. Libby had told him to stay away from Mr. Walker. But she came in here all the time, so he couldn't be dangerous. Besides, he'd run off Mr. Bevins. In Sawyer's mind, that meant Mr. Walker couldn't be a bad man.

"It's okay to come in. I'll tell your mother I invited you."

Sawyer stepped into the room, stopping at the foot of the bed.

"My name's Walker. Remington Walker. What's yours?"

"Sawyer Deevers. And Libby ain't my ma. My ma's dead."

"I'm sorry to hear that." He held out his hand. "It's a pleasure to meet you, Sawyer. Excuse me if I don't get up, but I've had a bit of an accident." His smile was friendly.

Sawyer moved forward to shake Mr. Walker's hand. "'T'weren't no accident. Libby meant to shoot you. She just thought you were somebody else."

Mr. Walker laughed aloud. "So she told me. I guess I'm lucky she's not a good shot."

"You're lucky all right. Libby can't hit nothin' she aims at. She prob'ly meant to kill you, which is why you're still alive." He sat on the chair next to the bed.

Mr. Walker's smile faded. "I thought ranches always had lots of men around the place. Why haven't I seen anyone else around?"

"McGregor, he's with the sheep. Ronald Aberdeen too. The others were all let go. Libby can't afford to pay more help. Things've been kinda hard 'round here since my dad died."

"Your dad worked here?"

Sawyer dropped his gaze to the floor. "He was foreman for Miz Blue and Libby. He froze up on Bear Mountain last winter, lookin' for the sheep Mr. Bevins run off." He squeezed his hands into tight fists. "It's Mr. Bevins's fault my dad's dead, and someday I'm gonna get him for it."

Remington empathized with the boy. He knew what it meant to lose a father. He also knew what it was like to want revenge.

Hoping to divert Sawyer's thoughts, Remington asked, "Have you been taking care of my horse for me?"

Sawyer's brown eyes grew wide, all traces of anger disappearing. "I sure have. He's about the best horse I've ever seen. What's his name?"

"Sundown. I've had him a long time. Raised him from a colt. I wouldn't want anything to happen to him. I'll tell you what, Sawyer. You take good care of him for me while I'm laid up here, and I'll pay you fifty cents a day."

"Fifty cents! A *day*?"

"That's right."

"Thank you, Mr. Walker," Libby interrupted from the doorway, "but Sawyer can't accept."

Both Remington and Sawyer watched as she entered the bedroom, stopping at the foot of the bed. She gave the boy a pointed look.

With his chin nearly touching his chest, Sawyer turned toward Remington. "I'll take good care of your horse, Mr. Walker, but you don't gotta to pay me for it. Thanks anyhow." With that, he shuffled away.

Remington felt bad for the boy. Wasn't Libby being a bit hard on him?

She seemed to read his mind. "I'm sure you meant well, Mr. Walker, but Sawyer should take care of your horse because it's the right thing to do, not because he can make money doing it."

"But I—"

"I'll see that he doesn't disturb you again." She shut the door behind her when she left.

Remington sighed as he leaned against the pillows. Sawyer had said money was short, and Remington figured the boy would take good care of Sundown. Was it such a terrible thing to pay him for his work?

"Sawyer should take care of your horse because it's the right thing to do, not because he can make money doing it."

Remington doubted Northrop Vanderhoff had ever done anything without considering the bottom line. How had that unscrupulous old man managed to raise a daughter with principles?

And how could an honest, kindhearted man like his own father have befriended Northrop Vanderhoff? How could his father have been fooled for so many years? How could he have allowed Northrop to drive him to such desperate measures?

All questions without answers. His father could not respond to them. His father was dead.

Weariness swept over Remington, and he closed his eyes, swearing even as he drifted into sleep that he would have his revenge.

Four

THE SUN WAS BARELY A promise on the horizon as Libby made her way toward the barn. The morning air was crisp, a lingering chill mocking the coming of summer, and dew lay heavy on the ground. The moisture sparkled like tiny diamonds scattered over the earth.

Libby loved mornings, especially this time of year, when everything smelled fresh and new. She never minded awakening early. She never minded the chores that awaited her. This was her time.

Raising her left arm toward the sky, she said, "'The heavens declare the glory of God; and the firmament sheweth his handywork.'" Quoting the verse made her smile. Praising God always had that effect on her.

When she pulled open the barn door a moment later, she heard the sound of whimpering puppies, obscured a moment later by a loud moo.

"I'll be with you in a minute, Melly." She set the milk bucket near the Jersey's stall. Then she walked to the back of the barn and knelt beside Misty. "How're you doing, girl?"

She stroked the border collie's head before picking up one of the black-and-white puppies.

"Look at you. If you're not a charmer, I don't know who is." She pressed the pup into the curve of her neck and jaw, enjoying the feel of his soft coat against her skin.

Melly let out another noisy complaint and kicked the side of her stall for good measure.

"All right. All right. I hear you."

Libby returned the pup to its mother, then stood and crossed the barn once again, this time entering the milk cow's stall.

"Getting a bit cranky, aren't we?" She patted Melly's fawn-colored neck.

A few minutes later, with the cow tethered near the manger, Libby pulled a three-legged stool up close. As soon as she settled on it, she leaned close to Melly's side and began to squirt milk into the bucket beneath the cow's udder.

Libby enjoyed this particular chore. The warmth of the barn and the rhythmic sound of the milk sloshing into a pail soothed her. Her thoughts could wander wherever they pleased. This was often the time she took her troubles to the Lord and asked Him for answers.

This morning her troubles had to do with Remington Walker.

Last night her patient had requested a crutch so he could get out of bed. Libby found one that belonged to McGregor and gave it to Remington. He hadn't tried to use it yet — at least not in front of Libby — but she suspected he would soon. She hoped he wasn't rushing things. A setback would delay his departure.

I don't understand it, Lord. He makes me nervous, having him around, though I'm not really afraid of him. Maybe

I should be. I don't know anything about him, and I know I shouldn't trust strangers. But something makes me think I can trust him. I don't know what it is for sure, but I feel it all the same.

She thought of Remington's slightly crooked smile, the way the corners of his eyes crinkled when he laughed. She remembered how his gaze followed her whenever she was in the bedroom, the intenseness with which he studied her, listened to her. She recalled the way his voice affected her, making her insides soften.

He was kind of handy to have around the other day. Even hardly able to stand, he ran Bevins off. God, what'll happen after Mr. Walker's well and gone? What'll keep Bevins from causing more trouble?

Nothing. Unless God willed otherwise.

Is that why Mr. Walker's here, Lord? Did you bring him here to help us protect the Blue Springs?

Her hands stilled as she leaned her forehead against the cow's side. She wished Aunt Amanda could help her make sense of things. The woman hadn't had an ounce of fear in her tiny body. She always seemed to know what to do.

Libby closed her eyes, remembering the night more than six years ago when she met Amanda Blue.

Olivia felt icy tentacles of fear wrap around her lungs and squeeze, making it difficult to breathe. She watched people filing down the aisle of the passenger car, taking their seats, and she silently begged them to hurry.

Go, *she ordered the train. Just go.*

She glanced out the window, staring at the darkness, wondering if he was out there, the man her father hired to bring her back. She checked to be sure her hair wasn't peeking from beneath the poke bonnet she'd tied on before leaving the hotel. She wished there had been time to dye her hair and scolded herself for not doing so sooner.

"Mind if I join you?"

Olivia turned her head and looked at the wizened face of the short woman in the aisle. She opened her mouth to say she'd rather be alone, but the woman spoke first.

"I'll be glad to put San Francisco behind me." *She sat across from Olivia and placed a carpetbag on the seat beside her.* "Too many people for my taste. My name's Amanda Blue. What's yours?"

"Oli — " *She stopped herself, remembering the mistake she'd made in using her given name before. In a flash of inspiration, she substituted the nickname her nurse had used when Olivia was a little girl, the name her father forbade anyone to use after he fired the nurse and sent her packing.* "Libby. My name is Libby."

"Nice to meet you, Libby. I'm on my way to Idaho. You ever been there? Pretty place. I got me a sheep ranch up in the high country. Best sheep ranch in the whole territory." *She shook her head.* "Pardon my braggin'. I can go on when it comes to the Blue Springs. That's my ranch. I've been missin' it real bad too."

Olivia had no response, but it didn't matter. Amanda Blue seemed content to carry the burden of conversation. As the train chugged its way out of the station and sped away from San Francisco, she regaled Olivia with story after story about the mountain country of Idaho Territory, about the men who worked for her, about the sheep and the lambs, about shearing seasons and lambing seasons. She talked on as the miles fell away beneath the churning wheels of the train, never seeming to notice Olivia's silence.

The darkness of night had cloaked the passenger car when Amanda suddenly leaned forward and covered Olivia's hand with one of her own. Her gray eyes were solemn, her expression understanding, her voice soft. "You're in trouble, aren't you, dearie?"

Olivia intended to deny it, but the words wouldn't come.

"Don't you worry." Amanda patted her carpetbag. "I got my Colt forty-five in here, just in case I need to do any persuadin', but my guess is, whoever you're runnin' from isn't on this train or he'd've made himself known by now. You're safe with me."

Strangely enough, the little woman made Olivia feel safe too.

"Why don't you come to Idaho with me, Libby? I got lotsa room on that spread of mine. Won't nobody come lookin' for you there."

"But you don't even know me, Mrs. Blue," she whispered, her throat tight.

"Don't have to know you t'see you need help, young lady. You come and stay just as long as you want."

Olivia glanced out the window. She had little money and no idea where she was going. She'd simply purchased a ticket on the first train out of San Francisco and hoped it would take her beyond her father's reach. But where was such a *place? In all the months of running and hiding, she had yet to find one.*

Could that place be in Idaho?

She turned and met the older woman's friendly gaze once again. "All right, Mrs. Blue, I'll come with you."

Amanda's smile was gentle. "Don't you worry, Libby. It'll work itself out, whatever your problem is. The good Lord'll see to that." She patted her hand again. "And you forget callin' me missus. Too highfalutin'. You just call me Aunt Amanda. It'll make us feel like we're family."

For the first time since she'd escaped her father's house one year before, Olivia smiled in earnest. "I'd like that . . . Aunt Amanda."

Melly kicked at the pail of milk, nearly spilling its contents. Reminding herself that she had more chores to do, Libby rose from the stool, grasped the heavy pail, and left the barn.

When she opened the back door to the house minutes later, she was surprised to discover Remington standing at the stove. He leaned on his crutch as he scooped ground coffee into the blue-speckled coffeepot.

Hearing her enter, he glanced over his shoulder. "Good morning."

"What do you think you're doing, Mr. Walker?" She lifted the milk pail onto the counter near the sink.

He raised one eyebrow, as if the answer should be obvious. "Making coffee." He flashed one of his crooked grins.

For some reason, his response irritated her. "I can *see* that." She took the spoon from his hand. "Go sit down. You shouldn't be putting so much weight on that leg. Do you want to start your wound bleeding again? That's just what I need, to have you laid up longer than necessary."

He didn't argue with her, and she suspected he was in a lot of pain. She watched as he limped over to the table and sat on one of the chairs. She thought to scold him a bit more, to warn him of the permanent damage he might do to his leg. Then he met her gaze, and the words died in her throat. She turned away, unsettled.

"I wanted to apologize for yesterday, Miss Blue."

She didn't look at him. "Apologize? Whatever for?"

"For offering to pay Sawyer. You see, he told me things have been difficult for you since his dad died and — "

"Sawyer shouldn't be bothering you with our troubles, Mr. Walker."

"The boy wasn't bothering me." He paused, then said, "And it sounds to me like you've got more troubles than you can handle."

Libby turned around. "We get by. Struggle goes part and parcel with ranch living."

"Then why do you stay?"

"This is my home, Mr. Walker. Where would you have me go?"

Remington watched as Libby held herself a little straighter. He saw the stubborn lift of her chin, caught the determined glint in her apple-green eyes. He admired her courage. After all, anytime she wanted she could return to a place where her every whim would be satisfied. And soon enough she *would* return to that life. Just as soon as Remington sent his telegram.

He frowned, not certain he wished that fate on her.

"Mr. Walker?"

He looked up as she drew closer to the table.

She placed her hands on a slat-backed chair. "I would be remiss if I didn't warn you about Timothy Bevins. He won't take lightly to what you did, making a fool of him in front of me. He's got a mean temper, and he fancies himself a cattle baron who's going to own this valley someday."

Remington felt a powerful urge to stand, take her in his arms, and hold her close while whispering words of comfort. If he had the strength, he might have given in to it. He was thankful he didn't have the strength. He wasn't about to be the second Walker to fall victim to a Vanderhoff. And no matter what Libby called herself, she was still a Vanderhoff. He would do well to remember it.

❧

Northrop stood at the window of his study and stared out at the Rosegate gardens. Beneath a gray sky, raindrops glistened on dark green leaves and lush lawns. In a few more weeks, the flowers would bloom, creating an explosion of color.

Not that Northrop cared about flowers. But he did take immense pleasure in people coveting something he owned. The magnificent rose gardens were no exception. His wife was responsible for the gardens that were the envy of every society matron in Manhattan, but Northrop wasn't the sort of man who thanked others for doing what he expected of them. Even if he had been, he wouldn't have thanked Anna for anything today.

Anger roiled through him. She had defied him, an unforgivable offense.

He heard the door open, but he didn't have to look to know it was Anna. No one else would dare enter without knocking first. Neither would she if he hadn't sent for her.

"Bridget said you wanted to see me."

"Sit down, Anna."

He listened to her footsteps as she crossed the spacious room and settled onto a chair opposite his desk. He waited, allowing the moments to stretch one into another, knowing she would grow more anxious with each passing heartbeat.

At last he turned.

Anna's face was pale, her gaze uncertain. At forty-five, she was still a handsome woman. Gray had yet to overtake her golden hair. Her skin was smooth, with only a hint of lines around her eyes. She'd even maintained her youthful figure.

"Have I done something to displease you, Northrop?"

"Now, what makes you think that, my dear?" He returned to his desk but remained standing.

Her face grew even more pale.

Northrop took perverse pleasure in watching his wife squirm. In twenty-eight years of marriage, they had played out similar scenes many times, and he never ceased to enjoy himself. He married Anna for the generous settlement her father bestowed upon the newlyweds and because her family's social standing was equal to his own. Anna had married him for love. Her one wish through all their years of marriage was to please him.

She seldom did.

Northrop picked up the folded paper on his desk. He knew the moment she recognized it. Her gaze fell to the floor.

"Why didn't you tell me about this, Anna?" He spoke softly, without a trace of the anger he felt.

"I ... I was going to, Northrop, but — "

"But what? What possible reason could you have to keep this a secret from me? Olivia wrote it almost a year ago."

Anna spoke in a near whisper. "It was addressed to me, Northrop, and there was nothing in it that revealed her whereabouts. I didn't think — "

"You never think!" he bellowed as he leaned his knuckles on the desk.

"Northrop ..." Tears pooled in her pale blue eyes.

He crumpled the paper into a ball. "Get out!"

"But — "

"I said get out."

She rose from her chair, then held out her hand toward him. "May I have my letter, please?"

He threw the wadded paper into the fireplace.

Anna stared at the flames, her eyes glistening, her chin quivering. She watched until only ashes remained of her precious letter, then she turned without another word and left his study.

The moment the door closed, Northrop sat down at his desk, swiveling the chair to stare at the fire. He thought of Olivia, the daughter whose beauty had promised to strengthen the kingdom of wealth and power he'd worked all his life to build, the daughter who betrayed him.

But he would find her. From the moment she ran away, he'd pursued her. Northrop had hired the best detectives his money could buy. He didn't care how long it took or how much it cost him. She would come home. She would obey him. She would bend to her father's will or be broken.

Northrop Vanderhoff never quit. He never admitted defeat. And Olivia knew it. Wherever she was, she knew her father was still looking for her. She knew he was searching, and she was afraid.

He grinned and lit his cigar.

Five

LEANING ON HIS CRUTCH, REMINGTON made his way outside. He paused just beyond the doorway to catch his breath.

The quick fatigue irritated him. By nature a man of action, he was impatient with his slow recovery. He wanted to *do* something.

To make matters worse, Libby had avoided him for the past two days. She sent Sawyer in with the water, salve, and bandages when it was time to dress Remington's wounds. Without the diversion of studying Libby, trying to ascertain her secrets, the hours dragged by.

Yesterday he listened through his open door as Libby and Sawyer held a Sunday worship service in the parlor. No preacher. No church building. Just the two of them, woman and boy, reading aloud from a Bible, then singing a couple of hymns, and ending with prayer.

There was a time in Remington's life when he would have joined them. There was a time when he loved and trusted God, as had his father and mother, as had his grandparents and his great-grandparents. But like his family's home in Virginia and his father's business concerns, another man's greed stole Remington's faith as well.

The sounds of hammering had drawn him outside. For the better part of an hour, he'd listened to the racket coming from the far side of the barn and wondered what Libby was building. He'd considered having a look, but then he caught sight of Sundown in the corral.

The gelding whickered a greeting as Remington limped toward him. Sundown thrust his head over the top rail and stomped in the dust, as if he too was impatient with his master's slow progress. Remington noted the horse's well-groomed appearance. Sawyer had been caring for Sundown as promised.

When Remington reached the corral, he stroked the gelding's muzzle. "Bored, fella?"

Sundown bobbed his head.

"Yeah. Me too." He glanced around.

The burnt-red barn was large and in good condition, the corral posts and rails sturdy, the yard swept clean. In the paddock, a small flock of ewes and lambs grazed, surrounded by a whitewashed fence. Blue Springs Ranch appeared to be a well-run enterprise.

He looked at the house. Although crude by eastern standards, it was roomy and solid. The inhabitants would stay warm in the winter and cool in the summer, something of prime importance in this country. The interior had been furnished to satisfy an eclectic taste. A Monet landscape hung in the parlor, looking out of place beside items that had undoubtedly been ordered from Sears & Roebuck or Montgomery Ward catalogs.

This ranch seemed an odd place for the daughter of Northrop Vanderhoff to have settled. What had brought her here? Why had she assumed another identity? Whom was she hiding from? Her father? Or someone else?

Remington gave his head a shake. He didn't care. He'd found her. That was the only thing that mattered. As soon as he could travel, he'd send his telegram, and once he collected his fee, he would return to New York. He had a promise to keep.

"Mr. Walker."

He turned at the sound of Libby's voice.

She stood near the corner of the barn. Her hair was swept back and captured in the thick braid that fell over her shoulder. She wore a man's work shirt, denim britches, and boots. A battered hat hung against her back from a leather tie around her throat.

"You shouldn't overdo," she reminded him.

"I won't."

She moved toward him with a natural grace, and it wasn't difficult for Remington to imagine what she must look like in satin and lace, her hair dressed with jewels.

"I'm surprised you made it this far. Are you certain you're not putting too much weight on that leg?" Her gaze moved down and then back again.

He rather liked her concern. "I'm certain." He motioned with his head toward the barn. "What are you building out there?"

"A new chicken coop. We had a coyote get into the old one a few weeks ago. He made off with one of our best layers."

Again Remington was struck by the incongruity of the situation. The daughter of one of the wealthiest men in America, wearing trousers, swinging a hammer, fighting coyotes, and shooting trespassers.

"I made lemonade this morning," she said. "Would you like some?"

"Lemonade?"

Libby nodded. "I bought some lemons last time I picked up supplies. You'd think they were pure gold for what they cost, but sometimes . . ." She shrugged off the remainder of her sentence.

"I'd love some. Thanks."

"Go sit in the shade under the tree there." She pointed toward the corner of the house. "I'll bring you a glass."

He watched her walk away. Her society friends back east would be scandalized by her inappropriate apparel, but he thought he could grow to like the fashion, should it ever take hold.

With slow steps, Remington made his way toward a bench that rested against the trunk of a tall willow. He sat, his leg throbbing. Libby soon came out of the house, carrying a tray with three glasses and a pitcher.

As she handed him one of the glasses, she asked, "What sort of business is it you do, Mr. Walker? What took you to Boise?"

"I raise horses." It wasn't a lie. He made his living as a private detective, but he still owned several mares and stallions whose bloodlines could be traced back to Sunnyvale, his childhood home. "My father once raised the finest Arabians in all of Virginia."

"I should have guessed." She glanced toward the corral. "Your gelding isn't the type of saddle horse we usually see around here." She brought her gaze back to meet his. "But you said 'once.' Is your father no longer living?"

Remington cursed the careless slip of his tongue. The less he said about himself, the better. Still, he answered, "He died fifteen years ago."

Fifteen years, but it might as well have happened yesterday. Fifteen years since his father—stripped of the JW Railroad, of Sunnyvale Plantation and its breeding stock, of everything Jefferson Walker had worked a lifetime to achieve—closed himself in his study, placed a gun in his mouth, and pulled the trigger.

All because of Northrop Vanderhoff.

Libby wanted to look away from Remington, but she couldn't. He appeared angry. Angry at himself. Angry at her. Yet she wasn't afraid. She wanted to comfort him, to offer him peace for whatever troubled his soul. Alarmed by her thoughts, Libby took a sudden step back, breaking the invisible hold he had on her. Lemonade sloshed over the rim of the glasses and onto the tray. "I . . . I'd better take Sawyer his drink. He's got to be wondering if I've forgotten him." She turned away.

"Maybe I could be of help, Miss Blue."

She glanced over her shoulder.

Remington rose from the bench. "I built a chicken coop myself when I was a boy."

Trust no strangers. She shouldn't forget that, no matter how much time had passed.

"Please," he said with a slight shrug. "Allow me to help." His gradual smile erased the effects of his frown.

Be not forgetful to entertain strangers: for thereby some have entertained angels unawares.

The words from the book of Hebrews echoed in her mind, but in her heart, she knew Remington Walker was no angel. In truth, she feared he posed a more serious danger to her than any she'd faced before: a danger to her heart.

"Miss Blue, I need something to do. Let me help."

Hadn't God protected her since the day she fled her father's house and a life of compromise? Couldn't she trust Him to continue to protect her?

"It's only my leg and side that's hurt, you know. I can still swing a hammer."

A sudden vision of Remington holding her in his arms overcame Libby. She saw his head lowering toward hers until their mouths could touch. She felt it, as clearly as if it were happening, and she wondered if she wanted God to protect her from this man after all.

"All right, Mr. Walker. You may help if you wish. But it's your own fault if you hurt yourself again."

Sawyer reckoned Mr. Walker might be of some real help around the ranch once he was good and healed, but from the useless way he swung at — and missed again — that nail, that time hadn't come yet. The thought had no more drifted into Sawyer's head than Mr. Walker smashed his thumb with the hammer. Muttered curses followed.

"Better not let Libby hear you talkin' like that, Mr. Walker. She'll wash your mouth out with soap."

Gripping his left thumb with his right hand, the man leaned his back against the side of the barn. "I'll remember that."

"You better. That soap tastes mighty bad."

Mr. Walker glanced in the direction of the house, as if watching for Libby's return. "How old are you, Sawyer?"

"Turned ten last month." He set a nail atop a board and began pounding it in.

"Have you lived here all your life?" Mr. Walker asked above the noise.

The nail in place, Sawyer sat back on his haunches. "Long as I can remember anyhow."

"Libby takes good care of you, doesn't she? You like her a lot."

"I reckon we take care of each other best we can, and God takes care of us both." He squinted at Mr. Walker. "You like her too. I can tell."

"What makes you say that?"

Sawyer shrugged. "I seen the way you watch her when she ain't lookin'."

Mr. Walker frowned as he reached for his crutch. "I think it's time for me to get off this leg. Sorry I couldn't do more, kid."

"It's okay. I like buildin' things." Sawyer watched for a moment as Mr. Walker limped away, then he grabbed another nail.

He wasn't wrong about Mr. Walker liking Libby, he thought as he set the nail in place. And he was pretty sure Libby hoped Mr. Walker would stay at the Blue Springs for a good spell. Sawyer had asked God to send Libby some help. Maybe Mr. Walker was His answer.

Six

LIBBY TOSSED RESTLESSLY IN HER bed. She couldn't rid herself of thoughts of Remington. Every time she closed her eyes, she envisioned him, and those visions were about to drive her mad.

Libby didn't want to fall in love, and she had no intention of marrying. Marriage meant bondage. Marriage gave men license for manipulation and even abuse. She'd seen it in her parents' marriage and in the marriages of many of their peers.

Husbands, the Bible said, *love your wives, even as Christ also loved the church, and gave himself for it.* Were there any men who loved like that? Perhaps. Perhaps somewhere in the world. But Libby would rather not take the chance of marrying unwisely.

Why was she even thinking such a thing? Had Remington Walker indicated he was interested in her as a woman? Certainly not. She was nothing more than a nurse to him.

Yet when she closed her eyes, there he was, watching her, smiling at her.

She buried her face in her pillow. "Leave me alone."

But the image of Remington didn't fade. She saw his raven hair, so desperately in need of cutting. She saw the blue of his eyes, the way his gaze seemed to look through all her barriers and into the depths of her heart. She saw the crooked curve of his smile, the dark stubble on his jaw at the end of the day.

Groaning, she rolled onto her back and stared up at the ceiling.

What's wrong with me?

In a short time, he would be well. He would return to Virginia. She would never see him again. That was best for everyone. She didn't *want* to see him again. She didn't *want* him confusing her. She had no need for a man unless he liked to work sheep. She was content with her life.

Libby was about to close her eyes when she realized her room wasn't as dark as it should be. Light flickered across the ceiling. Light that shouldn't be there. She sat up and turned toward the window. Beyond the barn, she saw flames.

"The shed! Not the wool!" She flew out of bed. "Sawyer, help me! The shed's on fire! Sawyer!"

She didn't wait to see if the boy heard her. Barefoot, nightgown flapping behind her, she raced outside, grabbing a bucket from the ground as she went. She rounded the corner of the barn and came to an abrupt halt. The full length of the wooden building was ablaze. No amount of water could save the shed or its contents. She could only pray the fire wouldn't spread to the other outbuildings.

Her eyes filled with tears as she let the bucket fall from her hand.

Half of this spring's wool crop was in that shed. Sacks filled with fleeces, each of them weighing close to four hundred pounds.

Sawyer's hand slipped into hers, but she didn't look down. She didn't want him to see her despair.

The wool had been scheduled for shipment at the end of the week. The heavy sacks would have been hauled into Weiser in the hired wagons, put on the train, and shipped back east. The money from the sale of those fleeces would have put the Blue Springs back on sound financial footing. She could have replaced the sheep they'd lost this year. She could have hired more herders. She could have —

"What started it?"

She turned to look at Remington through the haze of unshed tears. He'd wasted little time coming to help her. But there was nothing he could do.

"I don't know," she whispered after a lengthy silence. But she *did* know.

"You suspect Bevins?"

She nodded, unable to speak around the lump in her throat.

Two strides brought Remington close, and suddenly her face was pressed against his shoulder, his right arm circling her back. "Don't worry. It'll be all right."

It felt good to be held in his strong embrace. It felt good not to be alone. It felt good to be comforted. But after several minutes, reason returned. Libby took a step back. "I ... I'm sorry, Mr. Walker. I ... I don't know what came over me."

"It's understandable."

She took another step back, escaping his embrace, then turned to face the blaze once again. "We needed the money so badly."

She reached out for Sawyer and took hold of the boy's hand again, drawing him to her side. They remained there, the three of them, until the fire burned itself out, leaving nothing behind but smoldering remains. Then, before dawn could paint the horizon, they turned in unison and walked back to the house.

After Libby saw Sawyer to bed, she went into the kitchen and made a large pot of coffee. It was pointless for her to try to sleep. She had decisions to make, and more questions than answers.

What would Aunt Amanda do if she were here?

A sad smile touched her mouth. She could almost hear the spunky little woman. *"What do you do now? You pick yourself up and go on with what you got, that's what. You don't let nothin' keep you down, dearie. You just show the world what you're made of."*

But what *was* Libby made of? In the sixteen months since Aunt Amanda died, everything had gone wrong. Maybe Libby wasn't capable of running the ranch on her own. She'd had to let most of the herders go last fall. Dan Deevers was dead. Instead of buying new ewes and rams last year, she had to sell off more of her herd. And then there was Bevins.

What made her think she could make a go of the Blue Springs without Amanda's help?

"Can't sleep?" Remington asked from the doorway.

To be honest, she'd expected him to join her. Or at least she'd wanted him to. "You'd better sit down, Mr. Walker. You've already used that leg too much for one night."

He came forward, his stiff movements confirming the truth of her words.

"The coffee should be ready. Do you want some?"

He nodded as he settled onto a chair.

I felt so safe when you held me. I wish you would hold me again.

Fearing her thoughts, she rose and fetched two mugs from the cupboard. After filling them with hot coffee, she returned to the table, setting one of them in front of Remington.

"I know it's none of my business, Libby, but what does the loss of that shed mean to this ranch? How bad is it?"

His eyes were filled with concern, and she couldn't resist the pull of his words. Especially the sound of her name. Libby. He'd called her Libby instead of Miss Blue. "It's bad. Real bad. Half of this year's wool crop was in there."

"Half? Where's the rest?"

"I didn't have the men or the wagons to haul the sacks to Weiser after the shearers were done. I barely had enough to pay them their wages. So I sent what I could and planned to use some of the money from its sale to ship the rest to market. Now ..." Her voice drifted into silence.

"What does Bevins have to do with all of this?"

Her fingers tightened around her coffee mug. "Plenty."

Remington waited for her to continue.

"He wants to control the water from the springs that are on this ranch. Control the water, control the land."

"What about the other ranchers in the area? They must know it wouldn't be good if that happened. Why haven't they helped you?"

"There aren't any other ranchers. My nearest neighbors have a small farm about ten miles south of here." She shook her head. "The Fishers have even fewer resources than I do."

"I see."

Libby sat a little straighter in her chair. "Bevins made plenty of offers to buy the ranch, but Aunt Amanda wouldn't sell. Neither will I. We'll fight him to the last."

For the first time in fifteen years, Remington wanted something other than revenge. He wanted to give rather than take. He felt something besides hate. The foreign feeling left him on uncertain footing, and it was no doubt unwise. He needed to stay focused on his goal. He needed to remember what brought him to Blue Springs Ranch.

But he couldn't remember. Not when he looked at the determination on Libby's face, tear streaks still evident on her cheeks.

"I'll fight with you," he said softly.

Her eyes widened in surprise. "But you'll be leaving soon. You have no reason to — "

"I'll stay until I'm sure you and Sawyer aren't in any danger of losing the ranch. It's the least I can do after you nursed me back to health."

You're out of your mind. That's a promise you can't keep.

"And nursing you back to health was the least I could do after nearly killing you." Libby rose and walked to the back door. She pulled it open and stood framed in the opening, staring at the sunrise. The sun set her hair ablaze, shimmering red and gold. "I can't pay you, Mr. Walker."

His father would have said it was better to give than receive. His father had been a generous man with a compassionate heart.

"I don't expect pay, Libby." Using his crutch for leverage, he rose from the chair. "This is something I want to do."

Help her and then what? Return her to her father?

She glanced over her shoulder. Her green eyes revealed quiet despair. "Your family will be wondering what's happened to you."

"I don't have a family." A trace of bitterness worked its way into his reply.

Her gaze fell away from his. "Neither do I."

He studied her across the sea of lies and half-truths that flowed between them. Yet the lies didn't matter at the moment. All that mattered was the vulnerable but determined young woman who stood before him.

Seven

Northrop settled back into the leather-upholstered chair. "Well, O'Reilly, do you want the job?"

It was a rhetorical question. The man wouldn't turn him down. Northrop had offered him a mere fraction of what he'd agreed to pay Walker, but it was far more than any Irishman was worth, even though Gil O'Reilly came highly recommended.

"So, 'tis not your daughter you want me t'find, but the detective you've hired t'find her. Am I understandin' your meanin', sir?"

Idiot. "Yes, that's right."

"And does this detective have a name?"

Northrop felt like grinding his teeth. "Of course he has a name. Remington Walker."

O'Reilly let out a low whistle. "'Tis Mr. Walker himself you've got workin' for you." He rose from his chair. "I'd not be honest in takin' your money, Mr. Vanderhoff. Remington Walker was the best agent Pinkerton ever had. Though I've not had the pleasure of meeting him, I know his reputation right enough. He's got a nose for findin' people, he has. He'll find your daughter if anyone can, and when he knows somethin', he'll contact you. I'd swear to it on my dear departed mother's grave."

"Are you saying you don't want the job?" Northrop raised an eyebrow. "Not even if I give you a bonus in addition to your fee? Say, a thousand dollars if you find Mr. Walker by the first of September?"

"Didja not understand me, Mr. Vanderhoff? You'd be throwin' your money away t'hire me, what with Mr. Walker already on the job."

"It's my money, O'Reilly."

The red-haired Irishman shook his head. "That it is, sir. That it is." He considered the matter a moment or two. "I guess if you're determined t'throw it away, you may as well throw it my way. I'll take the job—and your money too."

"Good." Northrop grabbed a telegram off of his desk. "My agreement with Walker was that he would send reports every two weeks. This came from San Francisco over a month ago. There's been nothing since. I want to know why."

By the end of Remington's second week of convalescence, his side wound scarcely bothered him. He still couldn't walk without the crutch and the pain remained constant, but he moved faster and his stamina had improved. Perhaps Libby's cooking had something to do with his returning strength. Apart from her porridge, the meals she prepared were delicious, the portions generous.

"Where did you learn to cook like this?" Remington asked as he dished another helping of potatoes.

"Aunt Amanda."

He knew, of course, that she hadn't learned to cook at Rosegate. "Your aunt sounds like an interesting woman. Tell me about her."

Libby smiled. "She was interesting all right. There wasn't anything she couldn't do. She could rope a cow as well as any man. She sheared the sheep and helped with the lambing and patched the roof when it leaked. She rustled grub for twenty shearers in the blink of an eye, and she could shoot the ear off a cougar at two hundred yards with her Winchester." Libby shook her head. "Aunt Amanda tried to teach me how to do everything like her, but I'm merely adequate in comparison."

"I'd say you learned at least a few of your lessons well enough." He grinned wryly as he spoke, rubbing his ribs with one hand. Then, as he spooned canned beets onto his plate, he asked, "Was she your mother's sister or your father's?"

"Aunt Amanda was . . . unlike either of my parents."

Not the whole truth, but not really a lie.

Libby pushed the food around her plate with her fork, obviously troubled by either his question or her reply. Perhaps both.

She doesn't want to lie to me. The thought heartened him. "I wish I could have met your aunt."

She glanced up. "I wish you could have met her too. Aunt Amanda was special."

Libby had the most unusual eyes. Remington had never seen eyes that shade of green before. Once again, he thought that Northrop hadn't received his money's worth for the portrait of his daughter that hung at Rosegate. Certainly the artist hadn't captured the goodness of Libby's heart or her spirited determination to care for herself and those she loved.

Libby was more than the beautiful girl in the painting. She was more ... more than Remington could have imagined.

Libby felt a blush rising in her cheeks as Remington continued to stare, his gaze intense and thoughtful. She felt as if he could see right into her mind, as if he knew what she was thinking, what she was feeling. As if he could read all her secrets. She, on the other hand, could never guess his thoughts. Even when he smiled, he kept parts of himself closed off, in reserve, mysterious. She wished she could break through that barrier. She wished ...

She looked away from him, trying to calm the irregular beat of her heart, and turned her gaze on Sawyer. "I'm going up to Tyler Creek tomorrow."

The boy brightened. "How long'll we be gone?"

"I'm going alone. You need to stay here. Melly needs milking, and someone has to keep an eye on Misty and her pups too."

"But—"

"Don't argue, Sawyer."

"What's at Tyler Creek?" Remington asked.

"The flock. Tyler Creek's part of our summer range. I think McGregor and Ronald should know what's happened here." She sighed. "Losing the wool could mean I won't be able to pay them their wages. Not for quite a spell. They should have the choice to stay or go elsewhere."

Remington frowned. "I'm not sure you should be riding up there by yourself."

"What alternative do I have, Mr. Walker?"

"I could go with you."

She felt a strange tightening in her chest and knew she wanted him with her, but she shook her head. "You aren't ready to ride a horse. It's a long way up to Tyler Creek."

He leaned forward, his expression austere, implacable. "Then I think you should wait until I *can* ride."

She was tempted to agree. More tempted than she'd felt in a long, long while. She would like to wait until he was well and strong. She would like to let him take care of her, if only for a short time. She would like to depend on someone else for a change.

But she couldn't. Remington said he wanted to help, to stay until she and Sawyer were back on their feet. He hadn't promised anything beyond that.

Do I want him to promise more? No. She was better off alone.

Trust Me, beloved.

The words — almost audible in their clarity — made her insides tremble. *I do trust You, Lord.* But even as her mind responded, her heart knew the words weren't true. Not really. If she trusted God completely, would she hide the truth from this man? If she trusted Him, wouldn't she also trust the people He sent into her life?

Once again Libby shook her head. "I can't wait. I've got to go now." Was she speaking to Remington or to God? She wasn't sure. "I'm sorry. McGregor and Ronald should be warned. If Bevins manages to run off any more of our sheep ..."

Remington's scowl reminded her of her father. She closed her eyes, trying to escape the image of Northrop Vanderhoff, the determined glare of his eyes, his intractable demeanor. She could almost hear his condescending tone as he explained to her that he knew what was best for her. That she was merely a girl and unable to take care of herself, unable to *think* for herself.

But she *was* able to take care of herself. She *was* able to think for herself. She wasn't helpless. She wasn't mindless.

She opened her eyes and stared straight at Remington. "I can't wait for you. This is my ranch, and I'm responsible for what happens here." She rose and picked up her supper dishes. "My mind's made up, so there's no point in continuing this discussion. Sawyer, help me clear the table. Then you've got some reading to see to, young man. You haven't opened your primer in nearly a month."

Stubborn female. Remington moved the brush in brisk strokes over Sundown's back. *She shouldn't go into the hills alone when there's trouble brewing.*

But why did her decision rankle him? Libby had managed fine before he showed up. She wasn't his responsibility. He had other things to worry about. Getting well and sending a telegram were just two of them.

She'll be better off when she's back in New York. She'll be her father's concern then.

Thinking of Northrop Vanderhoff didn't improve his mood. He muttered a few choice words as he tossed the brush into a wooden bucket, then turned the gelding loose in the corral before heading back to the house.

Inside, he found Sawyer at the kitchen table, a book open before him. Libby wasn't anywhere to be seen.

"What are you reading, Sawyer?"

"Nothin' interesting." The boy closed the book, obviously glad for a diversion.

Remington pulled out the chair opposite Sawyer and sat down. "When I was your age, I read books all the time. Mark Twain and Henry Wadsworth Longfellow were two of my favorite authors."

"Mark Twain. He wrote *The Adventures of Huckleberry Finn*. Libby and I read that one awhile back. I liked it a lot."

"So did I."

Sawyer leaned forward and spoke in a low voice. "Libby likes to read poetry too." He wrinkled his nose in distaste.

"Poetry isn't all bad." Remington suppressed a smile.

"I guess." The boy shrugged. "Libby says the Psalms are Hebrew poetry, and I like them."

Remington thought of his father, reading aloud from the family Bible. Jefferson Walker had professed a strong faith, a deep love of God. When did that fail him? If he'd really believed, he never would have —

"You gonna join us for church tomorrow, Mr. Walker?"

"What?"

"Church. You joinin' us for church in the morning? We'll have a meetin' before Libby leaves. Sometimes a travelin' preacher comes through, but most of the time, we have church on our own. You gonna join us?"

"Well, I — "

"Libby says it's important not to forsake gatherin' together on the Lord's Day with other believers." Sawyer narrowed his eyes. "You *are* a believer, aren't you, Mr. Walker?"

Remington didn't know how to answer the boy. Did he believe in God? Yes. But he wasn't sure God believed in him.

Not anymore. Not since he'd turned a deaf ear toward the Almighty after his father's suicide.

"If you're not a believer," Sawyer continued, "we can pray and take care of that."

The last thing he needed was a kid praying for him. "Thanks, Sawyer." Remington stood. "I'll see how I feel in the morning." He left the kitchen as quickly as his crutch would take him.

The house fell into silence under the cloak of night. Libby sat in her room, a book of poetry by Thomas Moore open in her lap, lamplight flowing over the pages.

> *I feel like one,*
> *Who treads alone*
> *Some banquet hall deserted,*
> *Whose lights are fled,*
> *Whose garlands dead,*
> *And all but he departed.*

She closed the book, trying to blot out the loneliness that the poet's words stirred in her heart. She wouldn't think about being lonely. She wouldn't let herself abandon all she had gained. Not now. The price was too high.

> *I feel like one,*
> *Who treads alone . . .*

She extinguished the lamp and closed her eyes, but the words of the poem prevented slumber from bringing solace as her thoughts were dragged backward in time.

"You've kept us waiting," Northrop announced as Olivia entered his study.

Her mother was in the room, seated in her usual chair off to the left of Northrop's massive desk. Olivia took the chair on the right, as she always did for these meetings with her father.

"I'm sorry." She didn't give an explanation for her delay. Her father wouldn't care.

"I have important news, Olivia. You're to be married this summer."

"Married?" She glanced toward her mother.

Anna's compassionate gaze met hers briefly, then fell away. Olivia looked at her father again. "To whom?"

"Gregory James."

Olivia's heart thundered in protest. Gregory James, a railroad magnate as rich as Midas, was thirty-five years older than Olivia. Worse still, it was whispered that he was a drunkard and a womanizer who had flaunted his many mistresses in front of his now deceased wife.

"Northrop"—her mother spoke hesitantly—"Olivia is only seventeen. Isn't there someone—"

"She'll be eighteen next month, and it's time she married. This union will give Vanderhoff Shipping the access it needs to the South. We've intended to own such a railroad for years, and when James dies, it will be ours. It's an opportunity I cannot ignore."

Olivia suddenly saw herself as she would be in another twenty years, a replica of her mother, weighed down with sorrow. "I cannot marry him, Father."

Northrop turned wide eyes in her direction. "What?"

"I cannot marry Mr. James." Her insides twisted with fear. "He is old. He is cruel. He is godless. I cannot be unequally yoked with a man who defies God."

Her father rose from his chair. "But I have said you will marry him." He spoke with icy calm.

"I don't wish to be disobedient or to dishonor you, Father. But I must obey the Lord first. When I marry, if I marry, my husband must be a Christian. And ... and he must love me."

Her father turned toward his wife, his face flushed with fury. "This is what religion does. It warps the mind. I've told you not to fill Olivia's head with that rubbish." He cursed at her.

"It's not Mama's fault!" Olivia jumped up from her chair, frightened by the rage in her father's face.

Northrop rounded the desk with surprising speed. He grasped her by the upper arms, his fingers biting into her flesh. "I'll not have this impudence from you, girl. Do you hear me? You'll marry Mr. James. It's your duty to do as I command." He gave her a shake. "Do you hear what I'm saying, Olivia? I won't be disobeyed."

She wanted to ask him why he couldn't love her, why he couldn't love her mother. She wanted to ask him why he was so willing to barter and sell her as he would any other commodity that belonged to Vanderhoff Shipping.

In the end, all she said was, "Yes, Father, I hear you."

But she could not marry Mr. James. She knew then that she would have to escape. She didn't know how or when, but she would have to get away before it was too late.

Libby brushed tears from her cheeks.

I feel like one,
Who treads alone . . .

"Father God, help me. I'm afraid. I've been alone so long, I'm afraid to open my heart."

Eight

REMINGTON WATCHED AS LIBBY SLIPPED her shotgun into the saddle scabbard and mounted the Roman-nosed horse. The white swaybacked gelding didn't look strong enough to get her over the first foothill, let alone carry her up to the high pastures where the sheep grazed.

As if Sawyer had read Remington's thoughts, the boy said, "He don't look like much, but ol' Lightning's the most sure-footed critter you ever seen, and he can outlast just about anythin' on four legs."

Remington found that hard to believe.

Libby looked at Sawyer. "I'll be back tomorrow evening. The day after at the latest." She frowned slightly. "You do your lessons and make sure Melly is milked on time. I'm counting on you."

"I'll do it, Libby, but I still think I oughta be goin' with you. Mr. Walker's right, ya know."

For the first time that morning, Libby met Remington's gaze. "I'm able to take care of myself. I've been doing it for years."

She didn't want to need him, he realized. She was fighting it every way she knew how. And as crazy as it sounded, Remington wanted her to need him. He liked the way it made him feel, as if he was doing something worthwhile.

"Be careful," he said in a low voice.

Something in her expression softened. "I will." She nudged Lightning with her heels.

Remington watched Libby and the ugly white horse disappear into the grove of aspens and pines, knowing he wouldn't rest easy until she was back again. He told himself he didn't want to lose his finder's fee, but it was a lie. His concern had nothing to do with money.

"I guess I'd better milk Melly," Sawyer said with an exaggerated sigh.

Remington nodded, but his thoughts were elsewhere.

He hadn't come to Idaho for altruistic reasons. Finding Libby was a means to an end. He shouldn't forget that.

Besides, once Libby was back in New York, she wouldn't be in danger. She wouldn't need Remington to look out for her. She would have nothing more pressing to worry about than what color gown to wear each morning. In the end, he would be doing her a favor.

He clenched his jaw, resisting his mental attempts to justify what he'd come here to do. Her name wasn't Libby, and she wasn't the niece of an Idaho sheep rancher. She was a Vanderhoff and, therefore, his adversary.

Or was she?

Libby cleared a bend and recognized McGregor's camp in the distance, a ribbon of smoke rising from the central fire. *Thank You, Lord.*

The sun rode the crest of the western mountains by the time she guided Lightning down the trail toward the camp.

The dogs saw her first. As soon as one sent up a warning bark, McGregor was on his feet. He raised an arm and waved when he saw her. She waved back, then nudged Lightning into a trot, closing the distance between them.

"What're ye doin' here, lass? I wasna expectin' ye until next week."

She eased back on the reins, stopping the gelding. "We've had trouble at the ranch." She dismounted and faced McGregor. "The wool shed burned to the ground last week."

McGregor's eyes narrowed. "How'd the fire start?"

"We don't know for sure."

"Was it Bevins?"

Libby shrugged. "It could be. He came to the house a couple of weeks ago and made some threats, but Mr. Walker ran him off. I'm not sure what — "

"Wait a minute, lass." McGregor put a hand on her shoulder. "Who's Mr. Walker?"

"It's a long story."

He took the reins from her hands. "Ye'll be hungry. There's supper in the pot. I'll see t'yer horse, then ye can tell me yer long story."

A short while later, with Libby fed and Lightning tethered alongside the team of mules that pulled the camp wagon, Libby told McGregor everything.

"Don't ye be worryin' yerself about the sheep," he said when she fell silent at last. "We've got the dogs t'warn us of trouble comin', and we'll be ready." He poured himself some coffee from the battered pot, kept warm at the edge of the fire. "But are ye sure ye can trust this . . . Walker, did ye say his name was?"

"Remington Walker." *Could* she trust him? She wished she knew.

"Maybe we should bring the sheep down off the mountain, at least until we thinka what t'do next."

"We can't, McGregor. We haven't the feed in the valley to see them through summer."

"I'd rest easier if I could keep an eye on ye and the lad."

"No, you must stay here. Sawyer and I will be fine." She didn't tell him Remington planned to stay on a while. "It's the sheep I'm worried about. If we lose any more of them ..."

"Ye leave them t'Ronald an' me, lass. We'll see that naught happens t'them."

Libby smiled weakly. McGregor would do his best, but would his best be good enough? If she lost the ranch, where would she and Sawyer go? The Blue Springs had been a place of safety for them both. It was their home, a place where they'd known happiness. Would either of them find happiness again if they were forced from the ranch?

Sawyer played with Misty and her puppies out in the yard as dusk settled over the earth. The boy's laughter, the dog's barking, and the whine and yip of the pups floated on the evening air through the open window. The sounds were strangely pleasant, but Remington hadn't time to be lulled by them.

He glanced around Libby's bedroom. He ignored the twinge of guilt he felt as he moved toward the sturdy oak dresser in the corner.

The top drawer held several flannel shirts. The second drawer contained two pairs of men's denim trousers. The third drawer contained feminine undergarments, accented with ribbons and lace. He grinned, both surprised and glad that Libby hadn't taken to wearing men's underdrawers along with the shirts and trousers.

The bottom drawer of the dresser contained more surprises — two dresses, one black, one the same apple green as Libby's eyes. The dresses were well worn and out of fashion. Remnants from her past.

In this drawer, he also found a gold locket wrapped in tissue paper. He picked it up, letting the chain slip through his fingers. It was the locket Libby had worn for her portrait. Had she kept the pearls as well?

He opened the locket and found tiny portraits of Anna and Northrop Vanderhoff inside. How often did Libby look at this necklace and remember what she'd left behind? Was she ever sorry she'd left Manhattan? Was he right that he would be doing her a favor when he notified her father of her whereabouts?

No, I won't be doing her a favor. He frowned as he rewrapped the locket in the tissue paper and returned it to the drawer. *She'll hate me once she knows what I've done.*

But it couldn't be helped. He owed it to his father to see this through. This was his one and only chance to seize the justice that had eluded him for fifteen years. Such an opportunity wouldn't come again.

Remington closed the drawer and straightened, his frown deepening as he tried to picture Sunnyvale and the life he'd known there. But it was Libby he saw in his mind, her face filled with sadness. She didn't want to return to New York. She didn't want to go back to her father. Could Remington blame her, knowing what he did about that man?

He cursed as he reached for his crutch and limped out of the bedroom, as if running from the accusation he could already see in her eyes.

Anna Vanderhoff heard her husband's snoring, even through the heavy oak door that joined their bedrooms. The sound made sleep impossible.

Shoving aside the bedcovers, she rose and crossed the room to the large window. Holding aside the draperies, she stared down at the moonswept gardens, the one place where Anna felt a measure of real happiness. She often wished they were larger, so large she could lose herself in them forever.

Father, I ache to see Olivia again. Is she well? Is she happy? Is she walking with You? Keep her close, Lord. Keep her safe.

She turned her back to the window. Moonlight spilled across the floor, illuminating the door to Northrop's bedroom.

Oh, God. Don't let him find Olivia. He doesn't care what is right for her. He only wants to use her to satisfy his greed. Do with me what You will, Father, but please keep my daughter from a loveless marriage. Grant her a godly husband, I pray.

One more time Anna faced the window. She stared across the rooftops of the stately homes that lined Seventy-second Street. She stared toward the west and prayed that the men

Northrop had hired to find Olivia would fail. As much as she longed to see her only child, she wanted even more for Olivia to be free.

"I love you," she whispered, hoping the words would touch her daughter's heart and Olivia would know who'd sent them.

Nine

"COME ON, LIGHTNING."

Libby nudged the gelding with her heels, hoping to get a little more speed out of him, anxious to bring the ranch house closer that much faster. She told herself her urgency was because she didn't want Sawyer to worry about her, or because there might have been trouble of one kind or another while she was gone. She told herself everything except the truth.

She wanted to see Remington.

Throughout the previous night, she'd dreamed of enigmatic eyes and a smile that stopped her heart. She'd dreamed of warm embraces and fiery kisses.

He said he wanted to stay and help. But how long would he stay?

A few weeks. A few months.

Forever?

Her heart skipped a beat.

Forever.

Did she *want* him to stay forever?

The answer came with a sharp thud in her chest. *Yes!*

Libby pulled on the reins, stopping Lightning in his tracks. Breathing was difficult. Her pulse danced a rapid beat, and she felt light-headed.

"What have I done?"

She'd warned herself. She'd warned herself not to let this happen. Not ever. She hadn't thought it would. But it *was* happening. Against all good sense, against all reason, it was happening to her.

She was falling in love.

Libby closed her eyes and remembered the feel of Remington's embrace. It shouldn't have felt so wonderful. The memory shouldn't have stayed with her.

"There'll come a day when you'll fall in love." Aunt Amanda's words invaded her thoughts. *"The day will come when you'll not be afraid to give your heart away."*

Libby had told Amanda she was wrong. Libby didn't need anyone else in her life, least of all a husband. She could take care of herself.

"That's pride talking, Libby, my dear. And pride cometh before a fall, you know. At the very least, you'd best leave it up to God if He wants you to marry."

Marry? What was she thinking? When she ran away from her father's choice of a husband for her, she'd made the decision to remain untethered.

But if I truly love Remington ...

She drew in a ragged breath, then opened her eyes and started Lightning forward again. What did it matter what she felt? Remington didn't love her, and he wouldn't stay for long. He had a home and stables and wealth in Virginia. She had a home and sheep ranch and practical poverty in Idaho. He would ride out of her life as abruptly as he'd ridden into it, and when he was gone, she would look back and laugh at her foolishness.

Foolishness. I'll laugh at my foolishness. Libby repeated those words to herself often in the next hour. She repeated them so often she almost believed them. Then she arrived at the Blue Springs, saw Remington step through the back doorway, and knew she wouldn't laugh when he left her.

She would want to die.

Remington felt a surge of relief when Libby rode into sight. Strands of hair flew free of her braid. A fine layer of dust covered her shirt and trousers. Dirt smudged her right cheek and the tip of her nose. She looked tired and sweaty.

She looked adorable.

Leaning on his crutch, he hobbled to the corral. She glanced at him as she dismounted, then looked away as she looped the reins around the top rail of the fence and loosened the cinch on Lightning's saddle.

"Did you find McGregor?"

"Yes."

"Everything okay? They haven't had trouble?"

"No. No trouble." She glanced toward the house. "Where's Sawyer?"

"He took Misty and the pups down to the creek."

Remington leaned against the fence, taking weight off his bad leg. He thought of the dresses in the bottom drawer of Libby's dresser and wondered if she ever wore them. He watched as she lifted the saddle off Lightning's back and set it on the corral fence. In a swift, easy motion, she removed the sweaty blanket and laid it bottom side up over the saddle.

Then she slipped the bridle from the horse's head, replacing it with a halter and rope.

During his years in New York, working first for Pinkerton and then opening his own agency, Remington made use of his business connections and family background to gain acceptance among Manhattan's privileged set. Although he purposefully avoided the Vanderhoffs — easy enough to do with his moderate income — he knew his share of debutantes and society matrons. He sat at their supper tables and was entertained at their Newport estates and danced at their charity balls.

He even knew his share of unusual women, those who rebelled against fashionable mores. But none of them were anything like Libby.

He suppressed a chuckle.

As if sensing his amusement, Libby turned. Suddenly Remington didn't want to laugh. He wanted to kiss her.

And she *wanted* him to kiss her.

He felt that truth in the air like the crackle of electricity during a thunderstorm. He read it in her eyes as easily as he could read the stars on a clear summer night.

Libby moved to the opposite side of the horse, hiding herself from his view, breaking the spell. Lucky for him. Who knew what stupid thing he might have done otherwise?

He cleared his throat. "I've got stew for supper. I'd better check on it." He started away.

"Remington."

He stopped and glanced over his shoulder.

"Thank you," she said softly.

"For what?"

"For watching after the place while I was gone. For keeping an eye on Sawyer." She shrugged. "For staying to help."

The desire to kiss her returned with a vengeance.

She offered a tentative smile. "It's nice to have someone here I can trust."

Her words doused his ardor like a splash of cold water in the face. Trust him? She didn't know how wrong she was.

"I'll check on our supper," he replied gruffly, angry at himself, but even more angry at Libby. Angry at her for being born a Vanderhoff.

I won't love him. It would be the most foolish thing I've ever done. Libby looked at Remington across the supper table. *He'll leave soon. Perhaps in a week, maybe two. I won't love him. I won't.*

Lifting her chin for courage, she forced herself to speak. "You must miss your home, Mr. Walker. It shouldn't be long now before you can ride."

"My home," he repeated softly. There was a subtle change in his expression, a change she couldn't quite read. "You mean Sunnyvale."

"Sunnyvale. It sounds lovely."

"It was beautiful ... before the war."

Bitterness? Sadness? What was it she heard in his voice?

"Yes, I'd like to return to Sunnyvale."

See? She was right. He wanted to leave. He was eager to leave. Heartsore, she glanced at Sawyer. "Have you decided on a name for your pup yet?"

"Yeah. I been callin' him Ringer 'cause of the white ring around his neck. He's mighty smart, Libby. He's gonna be the best sheepdog we've got on the place."

Libby picked up her fork. "He will be if you train him right."

She tried to smile for the boy's sake, but she was hurting. Hurting in a way she'd never hurt before. Longing for something she couldn't have and shouldn't want.

Her appetite left. "I'm too weary to eat. I think I'll retire." She rose from her chair. "Just leave the supper dishes. I'll do them in the morning."

Once in her room, the door closed behind her, Libby drew a deep breath. It was for the best. It was for the best he was leaving. She didn't want a man to love. She wanted only her freedom.

But her familiar protests no longer rang true.

Ten

TIMOTHY BEVINS TIPPED HIS CHAIR onto its hind legs, leaning it against the wall of the house as he stared at the cattle grazing in the distance. A warm breeze stirred the tall grass. A green carpet covered the valley now, but if this heat persisted and the late spring rains didn't come, the land would be parched before the end of June.

He cursed as he dropped his chair into place with a thud and rose to his feet. He needed *all* the range hereabouts if he was going to increase his herd. He needed those sheep to quit eating the feed his cattle could use, and he needed to control the springs that provided water to the valley. Once he controlled it, he'd be able to shut out ranchers like Libby Blue and farmers like the Fishers, who had settled alongside Blue Creek.

Spurs jingling, he crossed the porch and went down the steps. Swift strides carried him to the hitching post where his horse waited. He freed the reins, then stepped up into the saddle. Jerking the animal's head around, he spurred the roan into a gallop and headed west, toward Pine Station. He needed a drink.

Hang Libby Blue! Why was she so stubborn? He'd given her plenty of chances to sell, lots of opportunities to leave without trouble, just like he'd done for the old woman before she died. Now he was running out of patience.

He didn't know how, exactly, but he was going to make the Blue Springs his. He would have to get tougher with her. Stealing her sheep and burning her shed wasn't enough.

Cle

Libby spent the morning in the garden, weeding, hoeing, and watering. The growing season was short in Idaho, and the vegetable gardens were too important to ignore. Without the food grown there, she and Sawyer and the sheepherders wouldn't have enough provisions to see them through next winter, let alone to feed the shearers when they arrived in the spring.

She hoped the hard labor would clear her mind after another restless night, and for a while, it did. But eventually Remington drifted into her thoughts. Instead of the smell of freshly turned soil, she caught a whiff of his uniquely male scent, something very subtle, something very Remington. It was so real, she sat back on her heels and looked about, half expecting to find him beside her.

He wasn't there.

Once he left the Blue Springs for good, she knew she would still be able to close her eyes and remember everything about him. The way he looked. The way he smelled. The feel of his arms around her, her face pressed against his chest. Everything.

As if conjured by her thoughts, Remington came out of the house, pausing on the stoop. The other night she'd asked God to take away her fears, to help her open her heart. It seemed her prayer had been answered.

Libby dropped the short-handled spade and rose to her feet.

She loved Remington — and it didn't matter why she shouldn't. She did, and she meant to love to the fullest. She would accept every moment God gave her with him, and when he went away, she wouldn't let herself regret loving him.

During the previous night, Remington had decided he'd done nothing wrong. He was doing his job. He'd been paid to find Olivia Vanderhoff. Withholding information, twisting the truth, and telling outright lies went hand in hand with being a good detective. Libby would be better off because of his work. Even if he succeeded later in crumbling the Vanderhoff empire, as he'd sworn he would do, Libby would still be better off in Manhattan than she was here. So he'd told himself last night. Watching Libby's approach, Remington's heart called him a liar.

"Morning," she said as she stopped before him. "How's your leg today?"

"Better."

She brushed wisps of hair away from her face with the back of one hand. "I was weeding the garden. I've been neglecting it." She glanced back at the tidy rows, then returned her gaze to him. "Pine Station doesn't carry much more than basic staples, so we try to grow as much of our own food as we can."

"Pine Station?"

"It used to be a trading post. Later it was a way station for the stagecoaches headed north. Folks thought it might grow into a real town, but the stage route changed because of the railroad, and Pine Station never grew much beyond the saloon and general store."

He frowned, thoughtful. "I didn't see it on the map I bought in Boise City."

"I doubt it's ever been on a map." She laughed softly.

"Do they have a telegraph in Pine Station?"

She shook her head. "No. I imagine you'd have to go to Weiser for that, although I can't say for sure. I've never been there."

Remington suspected she'd never gone to Weiser for fear of her father's detectives. She remained as close to this secluded ranch as possible. But she forgot she needed to be wary, even here.

She hadn't escaped her father after all.

"Do you need to send a telegram?" she asked, drawing his attention back to her.

Remington shook his head. "No hurry. It can wait."

"I suppose I could send a message with Pete Fisher. He might be going to Weiser sometime soon, and—"

"It's not important, Libby. It can wait until I leave."

Her gaze fell away. "Yes … you can do it when you leave." When she looked up again, her smile was sad. "Do you feel up to a walk? I need to stretch my legs."

Remington wished he could drive away her sadness, but he suspected he was the cause, not the cure. And if he wasn't the cause of it now, he would be soon enough.

Libby led the way to the pasture where she kept a few ewes and lambs during the summer months. Some had injuries that needed attention. Others would be slaughtered for food over the summer.

Misty, followed by her growing offspring, came out of the barn and preceded Libby and Remington to the pasture. The black-and-white collie slipped beneath the bottom rail of the fence and herded the ewes and lambs into a tight bunch. At nearly six weeks old, the puppies seemed to think the herding was a game for their enjoyment. They gamboled into the midst of the sheep, scattering them. The air was filled with a cacophony of bleating and yapping.

"Sheepdogs, huh?" Remington chuckled.

Her spirit brightened at the sight of his smile. "We'll need to do some training when they're older." She whistled to bring Misty in.

"*Some* training?" He cocked an eyebrow. "That's an understatement."

Libby feigned a Scottish accent. "Me good friend McGregor claims these dogs be smart enough t'cook yer breakfast an' serve it t'ye, if that's what ye want of 'em, an' he willna let ye say otherwise."

Remington leaned against the fence, grinning as the puppies crowded around her, whining and wiggling, begging for attention. The look in his eyes made her go soft and warm inside.

Her breathing slowed as her gaze dropped to his mouth, wondering what it would be like to be kissed by him. She had to know. She needed to know. With a gentle sweep of her leg, she moved the puppies aside and stepped toward Remington.

What are you doing, Libby? Don't do this!

But she kept moving closer. Slowly. Ever so slowly.

It's going to hurt when you go away, Remington.

She stopped when only a whisper of air separated their bodies. She heard the crutch drop to the ground, felt the puppies scampering around their feet, investigating the strange object in the grass, but Remington's arms encircling her dominated her awareness.

He lowered his head. She tipped hers back and to one side, then closed her eyes. His mouth covered hers, the most natural thing in the world. She felt herself grow hot, grow cold. Blood pounded in her ears, yet she thought her heart had stopped. Her skin tingled. Her knees felt weak.

He might stay ... He might stay ... He might stay ...

He raised his head. She opened her eyes.

He might stay ... He might stay ...

He brushed her cheek with the side of his thumb. "Libby ..."

Her stomach tumbled.

He might stay ...

"I ..."

She shook her head. "Don't say anything. Please." She wrapped her arms around him and pressed her cheek against his chest.

"Ah, Libby." He rested his cheek against the top of her head. "You don't understand."

"You're wrong, Remington. I understand."

His arms tightened around her. "No, Libby, you don't. But I do."

Then he lifted her chin with the tip of his finger and kissed her again.

Eleven

BLACK CLOUDS BLEW ACROSS THE sky as evening approached, driven by gusts of wind that bent the tall pines into arcs and rattled the leaves of the quaking aspens and cottonwoods. A shadow blanketed the earth, making the whistling winds ominous. Minutes later, the lightning began, a thunderous display that brightened the heavens and shook the ground.

Libby and Sawyer ran to the pasture and, with the help of Misty, drove the sheep into the shelter of the barn. Then they led the skittish horses, prancing and whinnying in alarm, into their stalls and closed them in. Only Melly seemed oblivious of nature's uproar. The milk cow stood quietly in her stall, chewing her cud and flicking her tail, her doleful brown eyes observing the frantic activity.

Libby felt a flash of envy for Melly's calm. She wished she felt the same. Instead she was as skittish as the horses, as the black clouds that tumbled and crashed. She'd been unsettled ever since she and Remington kissed earlier in the day.

"We better hurry, Libby," Sawyer shouted from the doorway of the barn. "The rain's comin'."

Libby followed the boy outside, racing to beat the deluge. She didn't reach the house in time. In a matter of seconds, she was drenched to the skin.

Sawyer entered the back door ahead of her. "Wow, ain't it somethin'?"

Libby shook her hands and wiped the rain from her face. "Yes, it is." She would have corrected his grammar, but then she saw Remington, and the words died in her throat.

"Sawyer's right. That's some storm." He limped to the window and looked outside.

The kiss had changed everything . . . and nothing. In less than three weeks, he had become the center of her world. She loved him even though he remained a stranger to her. How was that possible?

He turned. "You're soaked." The hint of a smile curved his mouth.

"I know."

"You'd better get out of those wet things."

"Yes," she whispered.

Remington glanced at Sawyer. "You too."

The boy nodded and headed to his room.

"I made a fire." Remington's gaze returned to Libby. "I think it's going to be a cold night."

She couldn't form a reply, so she too nodded and left the kitchen, hurrying to her own room. As she leaned against the door, her heart pounded a rapid and unsteady beat. Tears burned the back of her throat.

Love me, Remington. Stay with me.

Once, long ago, in a different life, she had learned the fine art of courtship. She was taught the things a well-bred young woman should say and do when in the company of men. Her lessons were detailed, right down to the proper way to hold and wave a fan and how to light a man's cigar. She learned how to waltz and how to walk and how to sit. She learned how to flirt and how to sing and how to play the piano.

But she'd forgotten all of those lessons. She'd put that world — and the girl she had been — behind her. When she donned a flannel shirt and denim trousers and became a sheep rancher, she forgot how to be a woman, at least the kind of woman who could charm a man.

Her eyes flicked toward the dresser in the corner of her room.

Would such a woman make Remington want to stay?

Remington added another log to the already blazing fire. The room was warm, and now that the lightning storm had passed, the sound of the rain upon the roof was peaceful.

But Remington didn't feel peaceful. He kept berating himself for complicating things with a kiss.

He didn't deny Libby was special in countless ways — feminine yet tough, generous of spirit, tenderhearted, funny, gentle, determined — but he couldn't fall victim to all the things he found appealing about her. He had to stay focused on the future, on his goal. There was no room in his life for a woman, particularly not *this* woman.

Wearily he sank onto the sofa, staring at the orange and yellow flames in the fireplace while his thoughts drifted.

Remington had enjoyed a reckless, carefree youth, unaware of his father's burgeoning debt. At seventeen, he went to college, more intent on having fun than on learning. He knew, of course, that his father endured hardship in the decade following the war, but there was always enough money for Remington to do as he pleased. JW Railroad, from all he was told, was returning to its prewar strength. Sunnyvale Plantation, although hard hit by the war and lacking in servants, remained in the Walker family, as it had for six generations. What could possibly disturb his carefree life?

How ignorant he'd been. How selfish and thoughtless. Maybe if he'd paid some attention to his father's worries . . .

Remington closed his eyes and leaned his head against the back of the sofa.

He remembered the shock of his father's suicide, of discovering that Sunnyvale and the railroad and all he'd known were gone. He remembered the fury that raged through him when he learned the part Northrop Vanderhoff played in Jefferson's destruction. He remembered swearing on the memory of his father to repay Vanderhoff in kind.

It took Remington over fourteen years to chart a course for that revenge. He'd begun to think it would never happen, that he would have to resign himself to letting go of the promise made beside his father's grave. But the opportunity finally presented itself last summer, and ultimately led him to this parlor tonight. He couldn't allow his heart to soften toward—

"Remington?"

He opened his eyes, turned his head, and saw Libby standing on the opposite side of the room, wearing the green dress he'd seen in the bottom drawer of her bureau. Her hair, still damp, was twisted into a bun at the nape, caught in a net made of emerald satin ribbons. Her hands were clenched at her waist, and she watched him with an uncertain gaze.

He rose from the sofa, placing his crutch under his arm.

She glanced down at her dress, smoothing the wrinkles with the palms of her hands. "I don't ever wear this anymore, but I thought . . ." She gave a helpless shrug.

"You look lovely." Why did she have to be Vanderhoff's daughter?

Libby took a hesitant step forward. "I haven't had much occasion to wear a dress since I came to the Blue Springs."

"To live with your aunt."

"To live with my aunt."

How many more lies would raise the wall that separated them? How many lies before she despised him completely?

"It's a pity," he said. "You should be seen like this often."

It wasn't her fault she was a Vanderhoff, but that's who she was. He would hurt her because of it, and she would hate him when he was finished.

She offered a tentative smile. "Aunt Amanda said they used to have dances in Pine Station on occasion, but when the stage route changed and the railroad didn't come through, folks moved away, and . . ." Again she finished her sentence with a small shrug.

"Do you miss dancing, Libby?"

She shook her head, then nodded.

"Would you like to dance?"

Her eyes widened.

Remington glanced down at his leg, then set his crutch aside. "You'll have to come to me."

Her eyes rounded even more. "You shouldn't, Remington. You — "

"Come here."

Even as she obeyed him, she said, "There's no music."

"Of course there is."

She arrived before him. He smelled the clean scent of her rain-dampened hair. He saw the fresh glow of her skin.

Taking hold of her right hand with his left, he placed his other hand in the small of her back and drew her closer. "Close your eyes, Libby."

She did, her long lashes fanning above her cheeks. Her mouth was parted slightly, and he heard the quick breaths she took.

"Listen. Can you hear the rain upon the roof?"

She nodded.

"Can you hear the crackle of the fire?"

Again she nodded.

"It's music, Libby."

He drew her closer yet, then began to sway from side to side.

Sawyer peeked around the doorway into the parlor and smiled. Libby sure did look pretty in that dress, and there was something right about her and Mr. Walker holding each other like that.

Sawyer's dad used to say that God never meant for man to be alone. "I was blessed because the good Lord gave me your ma for a time. Boy, when you grow up, you find yourself a wife like your ma, a woman who loves God with all her heart, and you'll never regret it."

Sawyer had to suppose the same was true for Mr. Walker. God must want him to have a wife who loved God too, and there wasn't anybody who loved the Lord more than Libby. Leastwise, none that he knew of. And if Mr. Walker could make Libby happy, all the better. Sawyer loved her something fierce. For as far back as he could remember, Libby had looked out for him when his dad was busy overseeing the Blue Springs, and after his dad died, she'd sorta been like a mother to him. Now he reckoned God had sent somebody to look out for her.

Still smiling, he drew back from the doorway and headed for his room.

Remington ignored the needles of pain in his leg. The pain was worth it if he could hold Libby a little longer. When it was over and she was back in New York, he hoped this would make up for some of his deception. He hoped she would remember tonight and not think too harshly of him.

He rested his cheek on the crown of her head and breathed in the fragrance that was uniquely Libby Blue.

I'm sorry. I'm sorry I must use you this way. If it weren't for my father . . . If it weren't for your father . . .

As if she'd heard his thoughts, she lifted her head and gazed up at him, and as he stared into eyes filled with love, Remington knew he was a greater scoundrel than Northrop Vanderhoff could ever hope to be.

Libby found it impossible to breathe as Remington slipped his right hand from her back and pulled his left hand from her grasp. Then he took hold of her upper arms and gently set her one step away from him.

"I think maybe you were right. I'm not up to dancing." He turned and reached for his crutch, then made his way with a *thump-step*, *thump-step* toward his bedroom. At the parlor entry, he paused and glanced at her. "You do look pretty in that dress, Libby. You ought to wear it more often. The men hereabouts would be buzzing around you like flies."

Something fearful pricked her heart, but she forced herself to smile. "A dress gets in the way when I'm working."

"Yeah, I suppose it would at that." He stepped into the hall. "Good night."

Libby sank onto the sofa and stared at the dancing flames. She listened to the crackle of burning wood and the patter of rain on the rooftop and knew she would never hear them again without remembering the moment he'd held her in his arms and swayed with her to the imaginary music.

The loneliness of her future closed in around her while outside the rain continued to fall, as if nature understood the pain in her heart and wept.

Twelve

FOR THE NEXT WEEK, REMINGTON distanced himself from Libby. It was for her own good. He didn't like her thinking he was something he was not. So why had he followed her out to the barn this morning?

When he entered, Libby was seated on a three-legged stool, squeezing milk into a bucket. He must have made a sound. She looked up, and her hands stilled on the cow's udder. Her eyes widened with surprise.

"You're up early," she said after a lengthy silence.

"You too."

"I always am." She returned to her milking.

Remington watched the frothy white liquid spray into the bucket and wondered how a woman could look so fetching while seated on a stool and leaning up close to the belly of a cow. He'd always appreciated feminine trappings, yet he thought Libby looked more enticing than any society beauty he'd seen, no matter how elaborate the dress or how sparkling the jewels.

"Aunt Amanda said milking was the best way to start a day. It gives a body a moment of peace so she can think before the busyness begins."

"I'm sure she was right." He stepped into the stall. "I've never milked a cow. Care to show me how it's done?"

Her hands stilled a second time. "You want to learn how to *milk*?"

Why can't I have the good sense to leave her alone?

"Are you sure?" she asked softly.

"I'm sure."

"All right." She slid the stool backward, then rose. "Come over here and sit down."

He leaned his crutch against the wall of the stall and limped the few steps to where Libby waited. She took hold of his arm as he sank onto the short-legged stool. When he was settled, she knelt beside him, the straw crunching beneath her knees.

"The first thing you must know" — she took hold of one of his hands and guided it beneath the cow — "is don't yank. If you do, you'll only succeed in making Melly mad." Her hand covered his. "Squeeze firmly, starting with your thumb and forefinger and rolling downward with a gentle pull."

He felt the warmth of her body near his.

"Use your other hand too," she instructed.

She always smelled clean and fresh, even here in the barn.

"Now alternate. It's easier when you get a rhythm going. That's right."

Milk shot into the bucket.

Libby laughed. "You're a faster study than I was. I thought I'd never learn how."

The last remnants of his restraint slipped away, and he did what he'd been wanting to do for a solid week, the very thing good sense told him not to. He turned his head and kissed her cheek. Afterward he kept his forehead close to her temple, knowing she could feel his breath upon her face, wishing he knew what she was thinking, cursing himself again for not being stronger, for not staying away from her.

The barn grew hushed and still. For an endless heartbeat, neither of them moved.

"You'll go away soon, won't you?"

He thought of his father and the promises he'd made. "I can't stay here."

She turned to look at him. "I know."

"Libby . . ." He cupped her cheek with the palm of his hand. "You don't understand. There are things you don't know about me. You —"

"I don't care."

"You *will* care," he warned, yet he couldn't keep himself from drawing her against him and kissing her again, this time on the mouth.

When the truth comes out, you'll care.

But Libby didn't care about anything as long as Remington was with her.

She didn't care that day or the next. Not that week or the next. Not as long as Remington sometimes held her in his arms. Not as long as he kissed her when they were alone together. Not as long as she could pretend they had forever.

She felt a desperate kind of happiness, a temporary one at best. Remington would recover from the wounds she'd inflicted with her shotgun, but Libby wondered if she would recover from the wounds of a broken heart.

Thirteen

STANDING ON A CHAIR, LIBBY reached for the earthenware jar atop the cupboard. Her fingers closed around the narrow neck of the vessel, and she pulled the jar toward her, carefully drawing it close to her body before stepping down. She removed the lid and tipped the container sideways, emptying its contents onto the table. The smattering of coins mocked her. There were so few left after paying off her debts, and now that the remainder of the wool crop was lost, there wouldn't be more any time soon. With a sigh, Libby scooped the coins into her hand and dropped them into the pocket of her trousers, then she walked to the back door and opened it. Her eyes quickly found Remington and Sawyer, standing inside the corral. Sawyer was brushing Sundown's neck and chest while Remington leaned against the gelding's back.

She paused to look at the two of them — Remington so tall and strong, Sawyer small and wiry but growing fast. Remington was patient with the boy, always willing to talk to him, spend time with him, and Sawyer's affection for the man was obvious.

He'd make a wonderful father.

Her heart skipped a beat.

·mington's child.

She imagined herself holding an infant in her arms, Remington standing beside them.

Oh, but that wasn't to be. There was no point in wanting the impossible.

With quick strides, she crossed the yard to the corral. Remington and Sawyer turned.

Libby deliberately set her gaze on the boy. "I'm going into Pine Station for supplies. McGregor will be expecting us soon."

"I'd like to ride into Pine Station with you," Remington said.

Again her traitorous heart skipped a beat. Remington grew stronger every day. Although the pain from his leg wound was still fierce at times, he could now walk without the aid of his crutch. Soon he would be able to ride again. *When are you going away? How long do I have before you go?* She drew a shaky breath. "You should stay here and rest. Sawyer can go along to help me."

"I'm plenty rested, Libby."

Her brief flash of self-preservation vanished. She wanted him with her every moment of the day, and she was too greedy to let this opportunity slip away. "All right, if you want to come." She glanced at Sawyer. "Help me hitch the team to the wagon."

As the three of them set out toward Pine Station — Remington with his rifle across his knees, Libby driving the team, Sawyer in the back of the wagon with his pup —

Remington told himself for the hundredth time how much better off Libby would be when she was back in New York.

He glanced at her without turning his head. She was leaning forward, her forearms resting on her thighs, the leather reins looped through her gloved fingers. She wore a floppy-brimmed felt hat, pulled low on her forehead. Her eyes were hidden in the shade of the brim, but he could see the splash of freckles across her nose and the firm set of her mouth.

She had more worries than a woman should have to bear. She shouldn't have to work so hard. She shouldn't have to live this hardscrabble life. Her father was one of the wealthiest men in America. She should be living in ease and luxury. After all these weeks, Remington had yet to discover why she had chosen this life instead.

He wanted to know why she'd run away. The reason hadn't mattered to him before. His questions up to now had been part of a game he played to satisfy his curiosity. But now her reasons mattered. They mattered because Libby mattered. She mattered too much.

"Libby."

"Hmm?"

"Tell me about your family." *Tell me what you were running from. Tell me why you're hiding.*

Her glance was quick and sparing. "I haven't any family. It's just Sawyer and me."

Another lie on the rising wall.

"Everyone starts out with a family. You told me you came from San Francisco to live with your aunt. What was your life like before you came here? Tell me about your parents."

She was silent for a long time, and he thought she might not answer him. Then she sighed.

"My mother's name was Anna." Her voice was soft, wistful. "Mama was a pretty, gentle woman, always kind to others, no matter what their status. Our servants loved her. Everyone loved her. Everyone except—" She cleared her throat, as if she'd choked on the words.

Remington waited for her to continue.

"I never liked our house. It was large and dark. I don't think Mama liked it either. That's why she spent so much time in her rose gardens." She stared off into space, as if remembering.

He pushed for more. "What about the rest of your family?"

"There wasn't anyone besides my parents and our servants. I wanted a brother or a sister, but Mama always told me I was enough, a special blessing from God. Sometimes she would come to my room late at night, after I was supposed to be asleep, and she would read to me from storybooks about magical places and people. Sometimes she read poetry, beautiful sonnets about ... about love."

"And your father?" Remington noticed the way her fingers tightened around the reins.

"My father didn't believe in fairy tales or storybooks. And he hated poetry."

Remington should let it go. He should let her be, but he couldn't. "What made you leave home, Libby? What made you come to Idaho?"

She turned, and he felt the hardness of her gaze upon his face. "Because I had no choice."

Tell me the truth.

"I lost my parents," she said, her voice cracking. She looked away. "I lost everything. I have no home but Blue Springs, no family except for Sawyer."

A long, pregnant pause followed. Libby had told him little, yet Remington understood so much more. He knew now, beyond a shadow of doubt, that Libby had run away from her father, that Northrop had hurt her, wounded her deeply. The worst thing that could happen to her would be for someone to return her to New York and her father's house.

Remington hated himself for what he'd done, hated himself more for what he had yet to do. But his promise to stay until Libby was safe from Bevins's attempts to take her ranch couldn't delay him from sending a telegram much longer. Once he could sit astride a horse for the hours it would take him to reach Weiser . . .

Libby slapped the reins against the backs of the horses. "Get up there!"

The team quickened its stride, and the wagon continued on toward Pine Station, the occupants cloaked in silence.

The sign above the Pine Station general store was faded but still legible from a fair distance. The store was housed in a long log building, single story and low roofed. The proprietors, Marian and Walter Jonas, were an elderly couple who'd come to the territory nearly thirty years before. They opened the way station when the gold rush was at its peak and miners were moving back and forth between camps. The couple stayed on after the boom, selling supplies to the farmers and ranchers who settled in the lush mountain valleys of Idaho Territory.

Next to the general store was Lucky's Saloon, run by a crusty old gold miner who had broken his leg when his cantankerous mule threw him down the side of a mountain. Somehow—no one knew exactly how—Lucky had managed to drag himself to Pine Station. He lost his leg to gangrene, but he always figured he was lucky to be alive at all and told folks so every chance he got. The nickname stuck, and everyone, including Lucky, seemed to have forgotten his real name.

All of this Libby had learned from Amanda during Libby's first year at the Blue Springs.

"Pine Station?" Remington asked as the wagon crested the hill and the two buildings came into view.

They were the first words either of them had spoken for over an hour.

She nodded, her throat tight with warring emotions. She wished Remington had never asked about her parents. The questions brought up too many memories. They reminded her why she left New York and why she could never leave Idaho. She remembered why she never meant to fall in love.

She glanced sideways at Remington and tried to tell herself she was mistaken about her feelings for him. It wasn't love she felt; it was loneliness.

But in her heart, she knew the truth.

"Libby, ain't that Mr. Bevins's horse?" Sawyer asked.

She spied the piebald tied to the hitching rail in front of the saloon. "Yes. It's his horse." She drew back on the reins. "At least we know he's not at the ranch causing trouble."

When the wagon stopped, Libby set the brake, then looped the reins around the brake handle and hopped to the ground.

"Leave Ringer in the wagon," she told Sawyer as she headed for the general store, not waiting for Remington or the boy.

"Mornin', Miss Blue," Marian called from behind the back counter.

"Good morning, Mrs. Jonas." Libby wound her way through the display tables, silently rehearsing her request. Marian Jonas could be a pain in the backside, but she was a decent woman at heart. Surely she would be patient a little longer, just until Libby could raise some cash.

"I figured it was 'bout time you were in for supplies." The plump woman offered a smile. "I could just about set my clock by Amanda's visits."

Libby nodded. "I remember."

"I got plenty o' cornmeal and flour and salt." Marian turned toward the large sacks stored in the back corner. "Imagine you'll want a bit of sugar for the boy."

"Mrs. Jonas." Libby paused, took a deep breath, then began again. "Mrs. Jonas, first I need to talk to you about payment for the supplies. I was hoping we could put them on account. You see, we . . . we had a bit of trouble out at the ranch." She held herself a little straighter. "As soon as we can market some more of our sheep — "

"Sellin' off your sheep's gonna make it hard to keep the ranch goin', ain't it, Miss Blue?"

She twisted, surprised to find Bevins standing near the wall of canned goods, hidden in the shadows.

"Your flock's been thinned down, from what I hear. How're you gonna pay Miz Jonas if you're broke?" His tone mocked her as he stepped forward into the light from the window.

Libby had thought Bevins was over at the saloon. She wouldn't have been so frank with Marian if she'd known he was here.

His smile was a sneer in disguise. "But then, maybe you plan on marryin' that fella you got livin' in your house with you."

Heat rose in Libby's cheeks as she turned to find Marian watching her with disapproving eyes. Before she could explain, the door opened and Sawyer and Remington entered.

"And you with that boy staying with you," Marian scolded in a low voice. "Have you no shame, Miss Blue?"

"It's not like Mr. Bevins makes it sound."

"I should hope not." Judging by her tone, Marian believed otherwise.

Libby squared her shoulders. "About putting our supplies on account. I'd be happy to trade mutton, if you prefer."

"Mutton upsets my stomach, so I don't suppose we'd have any interest in a trade." Marian glanced at Remington as he approached. "And Mr. Jonas has decided we can't extend any more credit. Money's short for everyone. I'm afraid we can't help you."

Libby heard Bevins's soft laughter but refrained from looking his way. "Thank you anyway, Mrs. Jonas." She turned to Sawyer. "We'd best be on our way."

"But, Libby —"

"Please don't argue with me, Sawyer." Tears threatened, but she was determined not to let them fall in front of Bevins. "We've a long drive back to the ranch." She glanced toward Remington, uncertain what to say to him.

"I need to pick up a few things for myself," he told her. "Why don't you wait for me in the wagon? I won't be long."

She couldn't do anything but nod and hurry out of the store before she lost control and began to cry.

Remington met Timothy Bevins's glare as the door swung closed behind Libby. Bevins was muscular and probably had plenty of brute strength, but Remington guessed he also suffered from a short fuse, a serious handicap in a game of wits.

As the large clock sitting atop a high shelf marked the seconds, the corner of Bevins's right eye began to twitch. A sheen of perspiration appeared on his forehead and upper lip. His weight shifted from one foot to the other, then back again.

"I suggest you keep away from Miss Blue and her ranch." Remington's words were deceptively mild.

Bevins's face turned red. "Who do you think you are, tryin' t'tell me what to do?"

"Who do *you* think I am?"

Again silence stretched between them. Remington waited it out. He'd known other men like Bevins, cowards who struck from behind, who picked only on those smaller or weaker than themselves. Bevins wouldn't take up Remington's unspoken challenge. He would turn tail, at least for now. A few minutes later, just as Remington had expected, Bevins swore beneath his breath, strode down one aisle, and slammed the door as he left.

Remington felt only a small twinge of satisfaction as he turned to face the proprietress. "Good afternoon. I'm Remington Walker."

"Hmm." Even though she had to look up to meet his gaze, she still managed to look down her nose at him. "I'm Mrs. Jonas. What can I do for you?"

"I need some supplies." His smile was congenial and hid his anger. "I'll be paying cash, of course."

He guessed correctly that Mrs. Jonas wasn't so offended she wouldn't take his money. Fifteen minutes later, he loaded the back of Libby's wagon with everything he thought might be of use to her.

Fourteen

"I shouldn't have let you do that," Libby said softly once Pine Station was behind them. "You shouldn't pay for our supplies."

"Why not? You've taken care of me when I couldn't care for myself. It's only right I do my part now."

Her throat hurt. "I don't know when I'll be able to pay you back."

"I'm not asking you to pay me back." He reached out and covered her hand with his. "I'm sorry. About what Mrs. Jonas said, I mean."

"It doesn't matter." That was a lie. It did matter. It hurt to be judged and wrongly accused. "We haven't done anything to be ashamed of." That much, at least, was true.

"All the same, it's time I moved out to the bunkhouse."

"But—"

"Doesn't the Bible you read say you're to avoid even the appearance of evil?"

His words stung. "Yes, but—"

Remington's fingers tightened around hers. "Libby—"

The crack of rifle fire cut him off. Dirt flew up in front of the horses. In the next instant, the reins were ripped from her hands as the team bolted into an uncontrolled gallop.

Libby screamed as the wagon hit a rut and bounced into the air, tossing her over the seat and into the bed. She landed on her back amid the supplies, barely missing Sawyer's head with her boot. The air *whooshed* from her lungs, and pain shot up her spine. She thought she heard another gunshot, but she couldn't be sure over the thunder of horses' hooves and the rattle and bang of the wagon.

Grabbing hold of whatever she could, she pulled herself to her knees and looked for Remington. He was leaning forward on the wagon seat, reaching for the errant reins.

Libby envisioned him falling forward beneath the runaway wagon. "Remington, don't!"

He vaulted forward onto the rump of one of the horses, his hands grasping the harness as his lower torso and legs bounced dangerously close to the flying rear hooves of the animal.

The wagon hit another rut, and Libby was tossed backward a second time. Her head smacked against a barrel. For a moment everything dipped and whirled, but she fought the dizziness, righting herself again.

She couldn't see Remington. The wagon seat blocked her view of the horses. Had he fallen off? How could he possibly hold on? What if—

She scrambled to her feet, whispering his name. The horses halted their breakneck gallop, tossing Libby forward. She grasped the wagon seat just in time to keep from falling yet again. That's when she saw him, sitting astride the lead horse, pulling back, sawing with the reins, slowing the team. A rush of relief filled her heart.

She glanced down at Sawyer. "Are you all right?"

"I'm okay."

"And Ringer?"

"He's okay too."

The moment the wagon stopped, Libby was over the side. As she ran toward the horses, she saw Remington slide to the ground, holding on to the harness to steady himself.

"Remington." As she spoke his name, he pulled her into his embrace, and she heard his heart beat against her ear.

They stood like that a long while before Remington said, "This is my fault. I shouldn't have provoked him."

"We don't know it was Bevins." She drew back and looked up.

"*I* know it was him." He raised his hand to cup the side of her face. His voice softened. "I'd never forgive myself if anything happened to you."

Her heart fluttered like the wings of a hummingbird, and she felt joy spreading a warmth through her body. He loved her. He'd never spoken the words, but he *did* love her. Maybe that meant he would stay. Maybe there was hope.

The blue of his eyes darkened. "It isn't safe for us out here." He took hold of her arm and turned her toward the wagon. "We'd better get moving."

⟡

With the sheep herders off with the flock, the bunkhouse had not been used for two months. It looked it too. Cobwebs and dust clung to everything, and a film of dirt on the window worked as good as any curtain.

Libby offered to clean the place for Remington, but he declined her help, needing time alone with his thoughts.

When he was with Libby, he forgot what mattered, he forgot why he'd come to the Blue Springs in the first place, he forgot just about everything except for his desire to hold her, to kiss her, to protect her.

But it's me she needs protection from.

Remington had made too many mistakes. He'd been careless. He let himself care for his prey. That was sloppy detective work, and he wasn't a sloppy detective.

He paused in his cleaning and leaned on the mop, taking weight off his bad leg. The pain had worsened tenfold since the wagon incident.

I need to get out of here. He rubbed his thigh. *I need to send that telegram and then put this place behind me.*

Libby wasn't Libby. She was Olivia Vanderhoff.

It is Mine to avenge; I will repay.

Remington raked a hand through his hair, wanting to silence the voice in his head. It was just one more reason he needed to get out of here. Ever since his father died, Remington had gone his own way with no thought of God, not considering if what he did was right or wrong in the eyes of the Lord. But since meeting Libby and Sawyer, he'd thought about his long-forgotten faith more than once, and he didn't like the guilt he felt because of it.

He cast a jaundiced look around the bunkhouse. This ought to prove something, his taking up residence in this dismal room with an uncomfortable bunk because he didn't want others talking about Libby, saying things that weren't true. But why should he care what they said? She wasn't going to live here much longer anyway. The talk wouldn't hurt her once she was back in Manhattan. Libby would be away from the gossip, and Remington would have his money and his revenge. That's the way it was meant to be.

It is Mine to avenge; I will repay.

Remington resisted the voice by tackling the dirt with renewed vigor.

That night Libby sat on the floor beside her dresser and stared at the miniatures inside the locket. She studied the hard expression on her father's face. She saw no laughter there, no joy, no love. She wondered if he was capable of loving others.

Her gaze shifted to her mother, to the sad-sweet expression on her face. That was how Libby always remembered her, sad and wistful.

"I miss you, Mama. I wish you were here to counsel me."

Lord, what is Your will? I used to feel like I knew what You wanted for me, but now I'm confused. Did You bring Remington here so I could fall in love with him, or is this a test?

Straightening, she looked down at the portraits, at this small link to her past, one more time. She brushed the miniature of her mother with the tip of her finger.

"I love you, Mama," she whispered. Then she closed the locket and put it away.

Restless, Libby left her bedroom. In the parlor, the fire in the grate burned low, and the red coals cast eerie shadows across the walls. The wind outside had risen, causing tree limbs to brush against the side of the house, whispering mournfully. It all seemed fitting for her mood.

It wasn't until she neared the sofa that she realized she wasn't alone. She drew a quick breath of surprise as she stopped in her tracks, staring at the dark shadow in the over-stuffed chair.

"Sorry," Remington said. "Didn't mean to startle you."

"I thought you were out in the bunkhouse."

"I came in to get another blanket and sat down to rest my leg. I must have pulled something today."

She sat on the sofa. "Is the pain bad?" She wanted to touch him, help him, comfort him.

"No," he replied, turning his gaze toward the fire. "It's not bad."

It wasn't Remington's leg but his conscience that bothered him most. He couldn't shake the image in his head of Libby being taken from the Blue Springs Ranch by her father.

"Remington?"

The soft plea of her voice drew his gaze back to her.

"You asked me earlier why I left my home to come here. I never answered you."

"It's okay." He was starting to think that the less he knew, the better. "It isn't any of my business."

"No." She touched his wrist. "No, I want to tell you. I . . . I was running away from my father." The hot coals on the hearth cast a red glow over her profile, the darkened room a perfect setting for the sharing of secrets. "My father decided I should marry a man who owned something Father wanted to acquire. My marriage was a business deal, and he didn't care what sort of man he'd chosen to be my husband. If I'd stayed, I would have had no choice but to marry against my will." Her voice lowered even more. "My father always gets what he wants."

No one knew this truth better than Remington.

"It was always that way," she continued, her voice soft and distant. "My father ran everything in my life. He chose my friends. He chose my clothes. He decided what I would do and where I would go, every minute of every day. The only thing he couldn't control was my faith in God. He—" Her voice broke.

She doesn't hate her father. The realization surprised Remington. He heard pain in her words but no bitterness. Resignation but no hatred.

Libby sighed, then sat a little straighter on the sofa. "I know from observing my mother what it's like not to be loved by one's own husband, to be unequally yoked with someone who doesn't share your beliefs. I saw what that did to her. I didn't want the same thing to happen to me. So I ran away. God's providence brought me here."

Remington took hold of her hand. With a gentle tug, he pulled her from the sofa and onto her knees on the floor before his chair. He cupped her face between his hands and claimed her mouth with his, wanting to wipe from her memory the pain he'd heard in her voice.

This was the daughter of his sworn enemy, and he cared for her far more than he should.

With his left hand, he freed the ribbon that tied the end of her long braid, then loosened the plait until the thick tresses hung freely down her back. Releasing her mouth, he trailed kisses across her cheek to her ear, where he nibbled her tender lobe before burying his face in her abundant rose-gold hair.

This was the daughter of his sworn enemy, and he meant to betray her.

I've got to stop this. I can't care for her. I've got to finish what I came here to do.

Holding her by the shoulders, he gently pushed Libby away from him. "It's late. I'd better get back to the bunkhouse." He rose from his chair, a bit unsteadily — unsure if it was because of his bad leg or the heady taste of Libby Blue — and walked away without a backward glance.

Fifteen

ANNA VANDERHOFF LET THE DELICATE yellow silk fabric slip through her fingers. "It is lovely, Mrs. Davenport, but I never wear this color. My husband prefers something more ... subtle."

"But it would be perfect on you, Mrs. Vanderhoff. With your eyes and your hair ... Why, you could find nothing better."

The woman was right. The yellow would be perfect. She wore this particular shade often when she was a girl, before her marriage to Northrop. The first time she did so after their wedding, he demanded she remove the dress and destroy it.

A tiny sigh escaped her as she pushed away the bolt of fabric. "No, I'm sorry. Please show me something else."

"Of course, Mrs. Vanderhoff." The dressmaker turned toward the doorway leading to the workroom. "Jeanette," she said to the young woman standing there, "please bring out some of the other silks."

While she waited, Anna's gaze returned to the forbidden fabric, and she felt bitterness burning hot in her chest. Why *shouldn't* she have a yellow dress if she wanted one?

But she knew why. Northrop would simply send it back to Mrs. Davenport. He would never allow her to wear it. The color was frivolous, he would tell her.

The shop door opened, causing the bell to tinkle. Anna heard Mrs. Davenport's gasp of surprise and twisted on her chair to see who had entered.

The woman was a stranger to Anna. Tall and attractive, she appeared to be no more than thirty years of age. She wore a graceful gown of India silk, the black fabric brightened with a pattern of pink and yellow blossoms. Her dark hair was mostly hidden beneath a large straw hat trimmed with pink ribbon and pink and cream flowers.

Mrs. Davenport hurried forward. "Good afternoon, Mrs. Prine." She spoke softly, but Anna still heard her.

Mrs. Prine? Anna continued to stare. Ellen Prine? If so, the "Mrs." was a lie, for Anna knew Ellen Prine was neither married nor widowed.

"I'm afraid your gown won't be ready until tomorrow," the dressmaker said as she placed herself directly between Anna and the other woman.

"But you sent word that —"

"I'm sorry. It simply isn't ready." Mrs. Davenport's anxiety was obvious.

The last of her doubts disappeared. This was Northrop's mistress. Anna rose and turned to get a better look at her.

At the same time, Ellen glanced in Anna's direction. The mistress's eyes widened and her back went rigid.

Anna understood. She felt herself stiffening too, knowing she was looking at the mother of Northrop's two illegitimate sons.

"Mrs. Davenport, why don't you check on that fabric for me?" Anna suggested, never taking her gaze off Ellen Prine.

"Well, I . . ." The dressmaker glanced from one woman to the other, then scurried from the room without another word.

Anna stepped around her chair. "You must be Ellen. I'm Anna Vanderhoff." She felt a surprising calm flow through her.

"I know who you are."

"It never occurred to me you might patronize Mrs. Davenport's shop, but I suppose it makes sense. This way, Northrop has only one bill to pay at the end of each month."

Ellen didn't reply.

Anna moved closer, studying the pretty, younger woman. No wonder Northrop was attracted to her. She had pale, flawless skin and a generous mouth; a long, slender throat; and a narrow waist. Her hair was a deep umber shade, almost auburn, but without quite so much red. She must have been no more than eighteen when she gave birth to Northrop's first son.

"I suppose it's surprising we haven't met before," Anna said at last. "After all, thirteen years is a long time."

"Yes."

"Do you love my husband, Miss Prine?"

Ellen looked surprised. "Love him?"

"I've always wondered, and this may be my only chance to ask. I may be dead and buried before another thirteen years pass. Do you love him?"

"Why would I stay with him if I didn't?" Her tone was defensive, haughty.

At one time, Anna had hated this young woman, sight unseen. Now she felt only compassion for her. "Why else would you stay? Perhaps because there is nothing else you can do. You are trapped as surely as I am, Miss Prine."

"My sons will inherit Vanderhoff Shipping when their father dies. He's promised me."

"Yes, I suppose they shall."

Ellen's color deepened. "You're no better than I. Northrop would have married me if he could. If not for you, I'd be living at Rosegate as his wife. No one would look down their noses at me then."

Anna lowered her voice. "You've paid an enormous price, haven't you? I am sorry for you. I'm sorry for us both." She glanced toward the workshop, certain the dressmaker and her seamstresses stood just out of sight, straining to hear the exchange between Northrop Vanderhoff's women. "Mrs. Davenport?"

The dressmaker appeared almost instantly.

"I've decided on the yellow silk after all. Please have the dress sent to Rosegate when it's finished." She glanced once more at Northrop's beautiful mistress. "Good afternoon, Miss Prine."

As the shop door closed behind her, Anna wondered if she would have the nerve to wear the yellow gown. Then she decided she didn't care. She'd bought it. That was all that mattered to her at the moment.

Cle

It was time Remington sent his telegram to Northrop. The longer he stayed, the deeper he would wound Libby, letting her think there might be more between them than a few kisses. It wasn't fair to either of them. He needed to go into Weiser right away, and it didn't matter to him that travel by horseback would be painful for his leg. It was more painful staying where he was. Each time he and Libby were together, the weight of his betrayal grew heavier in his heart.

His decision made, Remington was on his way to find Libby when a wagon carrying a man and a woman entered the yard. A moment later, Libby came out of the barn and hurried toward them.

"Lynette. Pete." She greeted them with a smile, the first smile Remington had seen her wear in two days. "It's good to see you."

The woman returned Libby's smile. "Pete's going into Weiser for supplies. I thought I'd come by for a visit, if I won't be in your way. Pete can pick up anything you need while he's there."

"Of course you won't be in the way. I'd love some company." Libby glanced at Pete. "Thanks for the offer, but there isn't anything we need."

Remington stepped forward into the morning sunlight. "I could use a ride into town."

All eyes turned in Remington's direction.

"This is Mr. Walker," Libby said as he came toward them. "He ... he's been helping me around the place."

The man on the wagon seat leaned down, holding out his hand toward Remington. "Howdy. I'm Pete Fisher, and this is my wife, Lynette."

"A pleasure to meet you." He shook Pete's hand. "Would you mind if I came along? I need to send a telegram."

"Don't mind at all. In fact, I'd be glad for the company. It's a long trip into town. We won't be back until nightfall, more'n likely."

"Thanks." Remington glanced at Libby. Her eyes were filled with a love she didn't try to hide. He hardened his heart to it. "I'll get my hat."

Lynette Fisher leaned against the side of the house and took a sip from the glass she held in her hand. "That boy has grown half a foot since the last time I saw him," she said as she watched Sawyer playing with Ringer. "You've taken real good care of him, Libby."

"I've tried."

"Lots of folks would've sent him to an orphanage. You've become a mother to him."

Libby smiled. "I *feel* like his mother. I love him very much."

"And what about that Mr. Walker?"

Libby's gaze dropped to the glass she held between her two hands. *I love him, too.*

"I thought maybe that's how it was," Lynette said softly.

"Is it so obvious?"

Lynette patted Libby's knee. "I've loved Pete for over twenty years. I know a woman who feels the same about her man when I see her."

"I wish you were wrong."

"Why's that?"

"Because he's not going to stay. He's got a place in Virginia. He'll have to return there soon."

"What's wrong with you going to Virginia with him?"

I don't think he wants me. She swallowed her pain and said, "The Blue Springs is my home."

"That's how I felt about leaving Iowa. That's where I grew up. It's where I met and fell in love with Pete. It's where we had our first farm." Her voice grew quiet. "It's where our only child is buried." She looked once again at Sawyer, playing with his puppy in the yard. "But Pete had a yearning to come west, so I came with him. We made this our home. I've never been sorry for that." Her gaze returned to Libby. "You could do the same."

But you weren't hiding from anyone. You didn't have to worry about what your father might do if he found you.

She was safe at the Blue Springs. Her father's detectives hadn't found her here. She remembered only too well her narrow escapes from Manhattan. Chicago. St. Louis. San Francisco. His detectives had tracked her to each of those cities.

But they hadn't tracked her to Idaho. They hadn't found the Blue Springs.

What if Remington wanted to marry me and take me to Sunnyvale? Would I go then?

Hope lightened her heart, but truth swiftly dashed it. Her father wouldn't let something as trivial as marriage stop him from taking her back to Manhattan. She'd known him to destroy men's fortunes for little or no reason. He would do the same to Remington. He might even do something worse.

No, she couldn't leave the Blue Springs. Not even if Remington asked her to — and he hadn't asked her.

Sadly she gave her head another shake. "I don't think he'll ask me to go with him, so it doesn't matter if I'd be willing or not."

She took a sip of the tea in her glass, feeling trapped for the first time since she'd arrived in Idaho.

Northrop opened the front door of the fashionable house, located a few blocks from his office. A maid appeared to take his hat and walking stick.

"Tell Ellen I want to see her in the drawing room."

"Missus Prine isn't at home, sir."

"Not at home?" He fixed a displeased glare on the girl. "Where is she?"

"I . . . I don't know, sir."

"It's Thursday. She knows I come for lunch on Thursday."

"Yes, Mr. Vanderhoff."

He headed toward the drawing room. "Then send the boys down to see me."

"Right away, sir."

Northrop went to the sideboard, lifted the top from a decanter, and poured himself a brandy. Glass in hand, he turned and swept his gaze over the room, noting the thick carpets on the floor, the large oil paintings with gilded frames on the walls, the groupings of upholstered chairs and sofas. The room was alive with color, very different from the somber tones of Rosegate. He'd never been sure how he felt about Ellen's decorating, but since he came to see her only two times a week, three at most, it didn't seem important enough to ponder for long.

The door to the drawing room opened, and Northrop turned to watch as his sons entered.

Cornelius, at twelve, was the taller of the two. He'd inherited his father's auburn hair, although Northrop's had long since turned stone gray. Unfortunately the boy inherited little else from either his father or his mother. Cornelius was a remarkably homely boy, thin as a rail, and meek. Nothing could make Northrop angrier than seeing his elder son shrinking back whenever Northrop raised his voice. At least Cornelius didn't seem to be dim-witted.

Ward, who would have his tenth birthday in two weeks, was quite the opposite of his brother, though no more gratifying. Short and brawny, with a face that was almost too handsome, he had a quick temper and an even quicker fist. He was led by his emotions rather than his head, a constant source of irritation for his father.

"You wanted to see us, sir?" Cornelius asked as the brothers stopped, side by side, just inside the doorway.

"Yes. Come in and sit down." Northrop pointed to a couple of chairs. As soon as they obeyed, he strode across the room to stand in front of them, clasping his hands behind his back. "Boys, I have decided it is time for you to leave this house and attend boarding school. As you know, you are my sons, but I am not married to your mother. You no doubt have been called names by your schoolmates. While the circumstances of your birth are not your fault, it is the truth, and people shall try to make you suffer because of it. But money can make people forget many things. You may be illegitimate, but you shall be rich if you do as I tell you."

Cornelius's face grew sickly pale. Ward's turned beet red.

"I will not have sons who grow up hiding behind their mother's skirts. You must get out into the world, fight your own battles." Northrop fixed Ward with a harsh gaze. "And you must fight with your head" — he pressed his index finger against his temple — "not with your fists. Do you understand me?"

Ward's eyes narrowed and his mouth thinned into a stubborn line while Cornelius swallowed, making his Adam's apple bob.

"Ward?" Northrop prompted.

"You can't make us leave Mother all alone."

"You'll do as I say."

The boy jumped to his feet. "You can't make us!"

Northrop's temper flared, but he kept a tight rein on it. What the boy needed was a man's belt against his backside. The school he'd chosen for his youngest son would know how to administer strong disciplinary measures.

The drawing room door swung open to reveal Ellen, her face flushed. "Northrop, I'm so sorry to have kept you waiting. I had an errand to run, but I thought I would be home before — "

"Another frock, I suppose."

Ellen glanced toward her sons, then back at Northrop as she freed her bonnet and removed it from her perfectly coifed curls. "Mrs. Davenport sent word my gown was ready. The one I ordered last month. The blue one you liked so much." She smiled at him, trying to hide her uncertainty. "Shall I have Cook serve our lunch?"

"In a moment. First, I must inform you of my decision about the boys. I'm sending them away to school. I have a couple of good boarding schools in mind. They should be ready to leave next week."

"Next week? But, Northrop — "

"On second thought, tell Cook to serve lunch at once. I must return to my office."

"Northrop, please. Can't we talk about this?" She stepped toward him and placed the palm of one hand against his chest.

She looked up at him from beneath a fan of thick eyelashes and tipped her head in a coy fashion.

It seemed Ellen would never learn that flirtation was useless in persuading Northrop to do or not do anything. Ellen was his mistress. She belonged to him, and she would do as he said or find herself penniless and homeless.

He gripped her wrist, intentionally squeezing until he saw the pain in her eyes. "No, my dear Ellen, we cannot talk about this. If you want your sons to inherit Vanderhoff Shipping, then you shall not interfere in how I choose to educate them. Is that clear?" He released her hand and turned toward the dining room. "Now, tell Cook we are ready to eat. I have work to do at the office and can't be wasting my time here."

Sixteen

PETE FISHER WAS A FRIENDLY fellow who seemed willing to carry the conversation in between Remington's monosyllabic responses. Remington was glad for the distraction. By the time the two men reached Weiser, he had learned considerably more about Pete and his wife, about Amanda Blue and the Blue Springs Ranch, about Timothy Bevins, and about the folks who lived at Pine Station than he had learned in the past five and a half weeks.

"Whoa." Pete pulled on the reins, halting the team of draft horses in front of the telegraph office. He looked at Remington. "I'll be over at the mercantile. I'll wait for you there."

Remington nodded. "I'll be along soon." He climbed down from the wagon, feeling stiff and sore after sitting for so long. He waited in the street until Pete drove away, then stepped onto the boardwalk. He paused again, staring at the door before him.

It's what you came to do. Get on with it.

Dragging in a deep breath, he reached for the doorknob and, after turning it, stepped inside.

The clerk looked up from beneath his green visor. "How do. Can I help you, sir?"

"I need to send a telegram."

The clerk slid a pencil and a piece of paper across the counter. "Write 'er down, just like you want 'er t'read."

Remington picked up the pencil and stared at the blank paper for a moment, then began to write.

```
Found Olivia. Send word of your date of
arrival to . . .
```

He stopped and scratched out what he'd written, then began again.

```
Found Olivia. Meet me in Weiser, Idaho,
July . . .
```

Again he scratched out what he'd written.

"Some folks have a hard time gettin' their words on paper." The clerk set another blank sheet in front of Remington.

He nodded and tried one more time.

```
Found Olivia. Well and happy.
```

Libby was well and happy . . . but she wouldn't be once her father arrived.

He saw her as she'd been two nights before, captured in firelight. He heard her confession. *"My father decided I should marry a man who owned something Father wanted to acquire. My marriage was a business deal, and he didn't care what sort of man he'd chosen to be my husband."*

Would she be forced to marry someone else of her father's choosing once she returned to New York? Would Northrop barter his daughter a second time?

The thought of her being unwillingly wed to someone who might be cold or cruel caused his heart to twist. She had fought hard for her freedom. Did he have the right to strip it from her? Could he hand her back to her father for thirty pieces of silver? Of course, Remington would be paid far more than that for finding Olivia Vanderhoff, but it made his treachery no less palatable. Not now. Not now that he knew her. Not now that he'd held her in his arms and tasted the sweetness of her lips.

He crinkled the paper in his hand, wadding it into a tight ball. "Sorry," he said to the watchful clerk. "I need to try one more time." When he had the clean slip of paper on the counter in front of him, he wrote quickly, decisively.

> No sign of Olivia in Idaho. Trail is
> cold. Suggest you forego further search.
> Walker.

Every word was technically true. Olivia Vanderhoff no longer existed. Only Libby Blue remained.

He shoved the paper across the counter. "Send it immediately." He paid the clerk and left the telegraph office before he could change his mind.

$\sim$

Gil O'Reilly waited while the hotel clerk studied the photograph of Remington Walker. Finally the man set it on the counter and met his gaze. "Yes, I remember him. He stayed here, but it's been some time ago. A couple of months, at least."

"Was he sayin' what his business was in Boise City, or who he was goin' from here?"

"Are you a bounty hunter? Is he a murderer or something?"

O'Reilly shook his head as he let out a chuckle. "Sure and there's no truth in that. Mr. Walker is a friend of mine, and I've important news for him. Trouble is, the man loves to travel and he's not much at correspondence, so I'm not knowin' where t'find him."

"You might try Mr. Wilen over at the bank. Seems to me I recall Mr. Walker having supper with him one night in the restaurant."

"I'll be thankin' you for your advice, sir." O'Reilly picked up the photograph and slipped it into his pocket. "I'll do that."

With the sending of that telegram, Remington threw away two hundred and fifty thousand dollars. A veritable fortune. He could have had his revenge against Vanderhoff. He could have kept the promise he made in Jefferson Walker's memory. With that money, he might have been able to buy back Sunny-vale, made it his own once more. There was so much he could have done with that money.

So why had he sent that telegram?

He pondered the question on the return trip, thankful Pete Fisher wasn't as talkative now. The answer, of course, was simple — once he was willing to admit it. He couldn't betray Libby. He couldn't send her back to her father, not for any amount of money.

Because he loved her.

It seemed an impossibility, given who she was, given who he was, but it was true. He'd thought himself incapable of falling in love. Although he'd enjoyed the companionship of many women over the years, none had made him think of love, perhaps because he'd been too filled with rage and bitterness.

With her gentle nursing of his wounds, with her devotion to Sawyer, with her faith in God and hope for the future, Libby had broken through his defenses. She hadn't only made him think of love, she'd made him feel it.

But what did that mean for them? She wasn't really Libby Blue. Her name was Olivia Vanderhoff. Her wealthy, powerful father was looking for her. Remington couldn't take her back to New York. What of his home there? What of his agency?

And there was the matter of his deception. Could he tell her the truth? What would she do if she knew what had brought him to the Blue Springs?

She might shoot me again. He grinned.

But his smile faded quickly. He was afraid to tell her the truth. He was afraid that if he did, she would despise him, and he wasn't willing to risk losing her. Not now that he'd found her. Not now that he'd found love. Perhaps one day, after they were married . . .

Married to Libby. He imagined her in all the different roles she filled — rancher, cook, housekeeper, nurse, surrogate mother to an orphaned boy — and optimism filled him. He didn't know why, but he was certain they would work things through.

His gaze lifted to the road, and he willed the team of horses to hurry. He wanted to see Libby.

Libby waved farewell to Pete and Lynette. "It'll be pitch black out before they're home." She glanced at Remington, standing beside her. "Look how late it is already."

"Pete didn't seem in any hurry getting back. He must not be worried about it. Besides, the moon will be up soon."

"I suppose you're right." She turned toward the house. "It was good having Lynette here for a visit."

"They seem like a nice couple."

Libby drew a deep breath, then asked the question that had been in the back of her mind since his return. "Did you send your telegram?"

"Yes."

"That means you'll be leaving soon."

"I'm in no hurry."

A spark of hope ignited in her heart.

Remington moved to the corral fence, leaning on it as he looked at the grove of trees. "I think you ought to cut down some of those. It would give you a better view of the road. You'd know sooner when someone's approaching." He glanced behind him at Libby. "You mind if I do some clearing? It would only take me a couple of weeks."

Libby's heart quickened. A couple of weeks. At least a couple more weeks before he went away.

"No," she whispered as she moved to stand beside him. "No, I don't mind. If you think you're up to it."

He turned slowly and gazed down at her, and she was sorry for the gathering darkness. She wanted to see his eyes more clearly. And she wanted him to see what she was feeling. She wanted him to know how much she loved him.

He pushed loose strands of her hair over her shoulder, then cupped his palm around her cheek in a manner that was becoming comfortable and familiar. She closed her eyes and leaned into his touch, letting her emotions peak and swell, like a storm on the Atlantic.

"Of all the women in the world," he said softly, "why is it *you* I want?"

She opened her eyes. He wanted her!

"Trust me, Libby."

She scarcely heard him over the hammering of her heart.

His lips brushed the tender flesh near her earlobe. His touch caused gooseflesh to rise along her arm. Her heart beat erratically, and she wondered if it might stop altogether.

But she didn't wonder for long. The thought vanished the moment his mouth moved over hers. Her legs felt weak, and she reached up with her arms and clasped her hands behind his neck, hoping to steady herself.

I love you, Remington. Stay with me forever.

She felt his fingers in her hair, felt them freeing her braid, allowing her hair to tumble down her back. All the while, his mouth continued to ply hers with deep, long kisses that made her feel as if she were melting.

I trust you. With everything I am, Remington, I trust you.

He drew his head back, although his arms still held her close. "Libby, I think we'd best turn in." His voice sounded strained.

"But you haven't had supper." She didn't want to be alone yet. She wanted him to go on holding her. She wanted him to kiss her again. She wanted him to tell her that he loved her.

"It's best if I just go on to the bunkhouse."

He'd said and done much the same thing two nights before, but something was different now. Libby didn't feel rejected this time. She felt protected and cherished.

"All right," she answered softly. "Sleep well, Remington."

"You too, Libby." He brushed his lips against her forehead. "Good night."

Seventeen

WITH HANDS BEHIND HIS HEAD, Remington lay on his bed and watched as early morning sunlight fanned out across the ceiling. He'd been awake much of the night, his thoughts too unsettled for him to find sleep.

Before he could marry Libby, he had to settle things back east. He had to close the door on the past. He meant to return the fee Northrop paid him up front. He would have to liquidate many of his assets to do it, but he would have no need for his agency or his home in Manhattan once he married Libby. He didn't need that life anymore. He wanted to live here at the Blue Springs. He wanted their children to be born and raised here.

Children with Libby. He smiled, liking the notion.

He would sell the shares in Vanderhoff Shipping that he'd purchased before leaving New York City. He wouldn't need them. For all he cared, Northrop Vanderhoff could become the richest man in the world. With Libby as his wife, Remington would be the luckiest. Once he cut the old ties, once the advance he'd received to find Libby was repaid, he could marry her with a clear conscience. Once that was done, as far as he was concerned, Olivia Vanderhoff would no longer exist. He and Libby would start fresh and new.

He thought of his father then, and for the first time in years, he didn't feel bitterness welling in his chest. Maybe God was right. Maybe vengeance was better left in His hands.

It occurred to him that the faith wrested from him by his father's suicide had found a place once more in his heart. It had returned stealthily, by degrees, so that he hadn't noticed until now.

Lord, forgive me for all those wasted years.

Perhaps, he thought, it was part of God's grace, mercy, and grand design that his love of the daughter of his sworn enemy would be what brought Remington back to the foot of the cross.

Thank You, Lord. Now if You would just show me the rest of Your plan . . .

Remington wished he could leave for New York today. The sooner he went, the sooner he could return and marry Libby. But there was much he needed to do here first.

He wanted to hire on a few extra ranch hands. They could begin clearing the trees that surrounded the ranch house and outbuildings. He didn't want Bevins taking Libby by surprise while he was away. Then he wanted to meet McGregor. Maybe the old sheep herder could tell him what needed to be done to get the Blue Springs on a firmer financial foundation.

But he wasn't going to worry about any of that today, he decided as he tossed aside the blankets and swung his legs over the side of the bed. Today he was going to ask Libby if she would marry him. The rest they could talk about later.

Whistling softly, he dressed and left the bunkhouse, crossing the yard and entering the back door into the kitchen. Within a short while, he'd stoked the stove, found a frying pan, and sliced bacon from the side of pork that hung from a hook in the smokehouse. Then he went to collect eggs from the chicken coop.

Libby's dreams throughout the night were of Remington. She dreamed of lying in his arms, of his kisses, of the look in his eyes and the caress in his voice. She dreamed of him saying he loved her and wanted to stay.

A beautiful dream, and she resisted giving it up.

But the smell of sizzling bacon pulled her from the pleasant slumber. It took a moment or two to realize she wasn't still dreaming.

She sat up and stared toward her door. Someone was cooking breakfast?

She tossed aside the bedcovers and reached for her wrapper. She slipped her feet into a pair of house shoes, then hurried out of her room and down the hall to the kitchen, stopping in the doorway to stare at the unfamiliar sight.

Sawyer was setting the table with Amanda's best plates. Remington stood beside the stove, flipping bacon in the pan and trying to avoid the splattering grease.

Sawyer was the first to see her. "Mornin', Libby."

Remington gave her one of his heart-stopping smiles. "Morning, Libby." He tipped his head toward the table. "Have a seat. The coffee's ready." He glanced at the boy. "Sawyer, pull out the lady's chair for her."

"Yes, sir," Sawyer replied with an enthusiastic grin.

Maybe she *was* dreaming. "What's this all about?" she whispered to Sawyer.

The boy shrugged. "Mr. Walker didn't tell me."

Remington delivered a steaming cup of coffee, placing it on the table in front of her. "Your breakfast will be ready soon."

"Remington, what on earth — "

He wagged a finger at her. "I'll bet you thought I couldn't cook anything but a simple stew."

"Well, I — "

"At Sunnyvale, we had grits for breakfast, but I noticed the Blue Springs doesn't stock it in their pantry." He clucked his tongue. "Serious oversight, Miss Blue. We'll have to remedy the situation."

She'd never seen him like this, and she wasn't certain how to respond.

"I hope you like your eggs scrambled."

"Yes, I . . . ." She let her sentence die as she watched him crack eggs over the hot skillet and whip them vigorously with a fork.

She resisted the urge to pinch herself. If this was a dream, she preferred to keep on sleeping. She was enjoying it too much. She liked watching Remington as he worked. She liked listening to him whistle. She liked the joyful gleam in his eyes.

"Your breakfast, mademoiselle." Remington brandished the plate with a flourish before setting it on the table before her.

Libby stared at the fluffy mound of yellow eggs and the crisp slices of bacon and the warm bread spread with huckleberry preserves, and her mouth began to water in earnest.

"It's wonderful." She glanced up at him, waiting for some sort of explanation.

He didn't give one. Instead he motioned for Sawyer to sit down, then followed suit. "Let's bless the food, shall we?" He offered one hand to her and one to Sawyer. When the circle was complete, Remington bowed his head. "Thank You, Lord, for all the good things You've sent our way. Amen." When he met Libby's gaze again, he pointed to her plate with his fork. "Go on. Eat."

With an amused sigh she did as she was told, taking a bite of eggs.

"Well?"

She swallowed. "They're very good." Then she grinned. "In fact, they're so good, Mr. Walker, I'm willing to offer you a job as cook at the Blue Springs."

His smile broadened. "That's a kind offer, Miss Blue, but I think there are other jobs around here that I could do better."

Her hand trembled as she picked up her coffee mug. Was he going to stay? Was he really going to stay?

She wanted to tell him that she loved him, but she felt a sudden shyness. The words seemed too intimate for the light of day, especially in front of Sawyer.

But she soon forgot her bashfulness as Remington regaled her and Sawyer with stories from his boyhood. A joyous mood filled the kitchen and swept Libby up in it. She laughed as he detailed the pranks he'd pulled on the old servant who had cared for him, and she shook her head when he confessed some of the trouble he'd made when he was at school. Before she knew it, the kitchen was ablaze with morning sunlight, and she realized how late it was.

"Melly must be miserable. I completely forgot about her." She started to rise from her chair.

"Wait, Libby. Let Sawyer take care of the milking this morning. We need to talk."

She felt the weight of breakfast in her stomach as she sank back onto her chair. What was he about to tell her? Had all of this been his way of saying good-bye?

Remington jerked his head toward the back door. "Go on, Sawyer."

"Yes, sir."

Libby held her breath as she watched the boy leave the table. When he closed the door behind him, milk pail in hand, the sound rumbled through the kitchen like thunder.

She touched a hand to her hair, remembering that she had not brushed it and that she was still in her dressing gown and house slippers. She flushed when she realized Remington was staring at her, the amusement gone from his eyes.

"I . . . I must look a sight," she stammered.

"Yes." A gentle smile returned to the corners of his mouth. "You *are* a sight, Libby. And I'd like to wake every morning to the sight of you."

She couldn't have drawn a breath to save her soul.

Remington chuckled. "I could have planned this better." His gaze swept over the dirty dishes that cluttered the table. "I should have at least picked some wildflowers."

"Wildflowers?"

"When a man proposes, he should give his intended a bouquet of flowers."

"Proposes?" *Can this be happening?*

Remington rose and came around the table. Favoring his bad leg, he got down on one knee, then took hold of her right hand. His gaze searched her face. "Will you marry me, Libby Blue?"

She looked at their joined hands. *Can this be happening? Can it be real?*

"I'm not a wealthy man, Libby, but I'm not impoverished. I can provide for you. Together we can make the Blue Springs strong again. I have some . . . debts and . . . and other obligations that I must clear up. I'll have to go back home and settle matters before we can marry." His hand tightened around hers. "But if you'll say yes, you'll make me a happy man. I won't fail you. I promise you, before God, that I'll be a good husband."

Libby wondered when she would awaken from this exquisite dream.

Remington drew her toward him until she too was kneeling on the floor. He threaded his fingers through her tousled hair, then said in a whisper, "Marry me, Libby."

Dear God, don't let me wake up.

"Marry me, Libby. Say yes."

"We would live here? At the Blue Springs?"

"Unless you want to leave."

She shook her head. "No. No, I want to stay." She swallowed hard, still feeling breathless. "What about Sawyer?"

"We'll be a family, Libby. The three of us. If that's what you want."

"Yes. Oh, yes, Remington. It's what I want. Yes, I'll marry you."

Anna knelt on the lush lawn and attacked the earth with her trowel, turning the soil, cutting the weeds. She enjoyed the feel of the mild sun on her back, the smell of the freshly turned earth, the buzz of bees as they hovered over budding flowers.

In another month, the temperature would climb and humidity would make being outdoors miserable. June, when everything came to life again, was Anna's favorite month of the year to work in the garden. June brought vibrant colors. The promise of new beginnings. Renewed hope.

The yellow silk gown had arrived that afternoon. Anna had placed it under her bed, still in its box. What was she going to do with it now? She sat back on her heels and looked at the sky. Cumulus clouds soared into the heavens. Like bushy hydrangeas.

She smiled as she returned to work. She and Olivia had often played that game, trying to decide what the clouds looked like. They would lie on the lawn, mindless of grass stains, and stare up at the sky, Olivia's head on Anna's stomach. Olivia would point and call out an animal or a bird or a country, and Anna would agree with her, even if Anna couldn't see it.

Of course, they never played such games when Northrop was around. Northrop didn't believe in filling a child's head with nonsense.

Olivia would have liked her mother's new yellow gown. "Oh, my darling daughter. I miss you."

Anna drove the trowel into the ground with sudden anger. How could she have been such a fool? Why had she allowed Northrop to be so cruel to his daughter? For years, Anna had hoped that her submissive behavior might win her husband to Christ. But now she wondered if her adherence to one part of Scripture had made her disobedient to others. How often had her actions denied her faith in God because of what Northrop demanded of her?

Was it pride that kept her living this way? Or was it fear? Fear of Northrop? Fear of the unknown?

After Olivia disappeared, it was too late for Anna to leave Northrop. Her parents were long since dead and buried. She had no money of her own, no place to go, and no one to go to.

Father God, what should I do? I want to be obedient to You above all else. And please, Lord, keep Olivia safe and free.

She dropped the garden tool into her basket, followed by her soil-stained gloves, then lay on the lawn, her arms stretched above her head as she stared at the sky.

"There's a horse!" she shouted. "And there's a giant strawberry!" Then she laughed, but it was the laughter of an anguished heart.

Fleetingly she thought that if Northrop were to see her, he would have her confined in an institution. Perhaps that was his aim after all these years. To drive her mad. Maybe he wanted to be rid of her, and this was his way of going about it.

But she knew it wasn't true. Northrop was proud of her, in his own cruel way. She had the background, the breeding, that a man needed in a wife. She could entertain and socialize with men and women important to Northrop, if only for his ego. He might keep Ellen Prine for his mistress, but he would never marry her, even if Anna was gone. Ellen Prine didn't have the proper pedigree.

Northrop kept both women because it suited him. No, if he'd wanted to be rid of Anna, he would have done so long ago.

She thought of the telegram that had arrived from one of Northrop's detectives. He'd failed too. He hadn't found Olivia. He'd advised Northrop to give up the search.

But she knew her husband wouldn't give up. He was not a man who accepted defeat. He would keep searching for Olivia, until the day he died if it took him that long. The cost was irrelevant to him. It was winning he cared about. Winning — and the blind submission of those who were his.

"Don't let him find you, Olivia." Tears spilled down Anna's cheeks. "I'd rather never see you again than have him hurt you."

◌

"You're gettin' married?" Sawyer looked from Libby to Remington.

Remington nodded, his expression somewhat grim. "What do you think about that? Is it okay with you?"

Sawyer thought that was a dumb question. "'Course it's okay. It's what I've been prayin' for."

"You have?" Libby said, surprise in her voice.

"Well, sure. You need each other. Anybody can see that."

Sometimes, Sawyer reckoned, grown-ups didn't have more sense than one of those sheep out in the paddock.

Eighteen

THE STEEP SLOPE OF THE mountain caused the horses to lunge as they made their way up to the plateau. Remington felt the strain on his wound as he stood in his stirrups and leaned forward over Sundown's neck. But when they reached the top, he decided the climb had been worth the added discomfort.

The plateau, with its bluff that fell away suddenly, provided a panorama of the surrounding countryside. Wide swaths of green grass covered the lowlands, a ribbon of water winding down the center. Rugged mountains, heavily wooded, stood sentinel on three sides of the valley. From this vantage point, Remington could see the rooftops of the house and barn at the Blue Springs.

"Look at the birds in that tree!" Sawyer shouted. "There must be a hundred of 'em."

Remington and Libby watched the boy as he ran across the clearing, stopping beneath the tall pine. Its mossy arms danced as blue jays, dozens of them, hopped from limb to limb.

Remington's gaze shifted to Libby. She wore a soft expression, one of tender loving, one that reminded him of her mother. Anna Vanderhoff had worn a similar expression when she told Remington about her missing daughter.

He suddenly wished he could tell Libby what her mother had said, about the love that had shone so clearly in her eyes. He wished he could give Libby that comfort, but he couldn't. Not yet.

Libby faced the bluff and pointed. "That's Bevins's spread over there. The house doesn't look like much from here, but it's as close as a person gets to a mansion in these parts. I think Bevins fancied himself a country gentleman when he had it designed. You'd never guess it was built for a bachelor with no children."

Remington found the large white house, far in the distance, set up against a hillside.

Turning and pointing again, Libby continued. "That's the Fisher farm down there, near the creek, and over that ridge is Pine Station."

"How much of this land belongs to the Blue Springs?"

"From there" — once more she pointed — "on up to the pass through those mountains. But the flocks are only here for a few months of the year, at lambing and shearing time. We summer in the upper valleys toward the lake country. For a good portion of the winter, we take them farther south. Not that we have to worry as much about the feed situation, now that our flock's so small."

"We'll buy more sheep."

"There's no money for that. Not after losing the wool crop. We'll stop selling lambs to be butchered and rebuild the flock that way."

Hearing the weariness in her voice, Remington laid his arm around her shoulder and drew her against his side. "We'll work it out."

She looked at him, and he saw realization dawn in her eyes. "I don't have to do this alone, do I?"

He shook his head.

Libby laid her head against his shoulder. "I wish you didn't have to leave, even for a few weeks."

"You won't be alone. I plan to hire more help before I go."

"We can't afford any more hands."

"You let me worry about that. I've got enough to pay wages for a few months. That includes McGregor and Aberdeen."

"Remington, I can't let you — "

This time he pulled her around to face him, tipping her head back so their eyes could meet. "Maybe *you* can't, Libby, but *we* can. This is our future. Yours and mine and Sawyer's. We're in this together, and we'll make it work together."

Tears glistened in her eyes, and it was as if he could look into her past, could see how frightened she'd been at times, how lonely. He wanted to make her forget it all. He wanted to make everything perfect for her from this day forward.

A tremulous smile curved the corners of her mouth.

Remington kissed the tip of her freckled nose. When he straightened, he said, "Now, Miss Blue, we've got plans to make. When is it we need to take those supplies up to McGregor?"

"Soon ... but, Remington, it's a long ride. Are you sure your leg is healed enough to — "

"Are you always going to fuss over me like this, Libby?"

Whatever she might have answered was silenced by a cry of alarm from Sawyer. Remington and Libby whirled toward the sound and saw a cloud of dust rising above the rim of the bluff.

"Sawyer!" Libby raced toward the edge.

Remington was only a step behind her. He grabbed hold of her arm, then looked down. With both hands, Sawyer clung to a large tree root that protruded from the cliff, and it looked as though he'd found a toehold on a narrow ridge below him.

"Sawyer! Are you hurt?" he called down.

"N–no. I . . . I d–don't think s–so."

"Hang on. We'll get you." He glanced at Libby. She was as pale as bleached sheeting. "Sit down," he said, afraid that if she didn't, she would be the next one to tumble over the side. Once she obeyed, he hurried toward Sundown. He removed the rope from the saddle, then led the horse back to the ridge.

"Sawyer, I'm making a loop in the rope and lowering it down to you. You grab hold of it and put it around you, under your arms. Okay? Do you understand?"

"Uh-huh."

"Lord," Libby prayed softly, "protect Sawyer. Don't let him fall. Send Your angels to hold him steady."

Remington would welcome the aid of a few heavenly warriors right about now. He twisted the rope, tightening the knots and testing them several times before he secured one end around the pommel of Sundown's saddle, then stepped toward the edge again and looked over.

"Here comes the rope, Sawyer. Don't try to grab for it. Let it come to you." He lowered the rope until it was within reach. "Okay. It's just above your right shoulder. Let go with one hand and take hold of it. Sawyer? Can you hear me?"

"I . . . I can't l–let go. I'm too . . . too scared."

The ledge holding Sawyer's feet began to crumble, tiny pebbles tumbling away.

Libby got to her feet. "Bring up the rope, Remington. You'll have to lower me down after him."

"What?" He turned his gaze on her.

"I'm small and light." Fear had left both her expression and her voice. "You and Sundown can get me down before Sawyer loses his grip and still be able to pull us back up."

He wanted to refuse her. He wanted to tell her he forbade her to go down the side of that cliff, risking her life. But he couldn't argue because time was too precious.

God, help us.

Libby leaned forward. "Hang on, Sawyer. I'm coming down. Just hold tight."

The hemp rope pinched the flesh beneath her arms through her shirt as Libby was lowered over the side of the bluff. Her pulse pounded in her ears, and she felt short of breath. If she was this frightened with a rope tied safely around her, she could imagine how terrified Sawyer must be, clinging tenaciously to that insubstantial root.

She forced herself to sound calm. "I'm almost there, Sawyer. Can you see me?"

"Yeah. Yeah, I c–can s–see you, Libby."

"Good. Just keep your eyes on me." *Jesus, help me reach him in time.*

She continued to walk down the face of the rocky cliff, her hands gripping the rope. How, she wondered, could such a slender bit of hemp support not only her weight but Sawyer's too?

"Here I am, Sawyer. I'm right beside you."

The boy bravely tried to joke. "I didn't have anywhere else to go, so I've just been waitin' for you, Libby."

"I know you have." She gave him an encouraging smile. "Now, I'll tell you what we're going to do. I'm going to wrap my arms around you like this." She slipped her arms around his chest, clasping her wrists. "You let go of that root and grab hold of the rope. Go on. Let go. I've got you."

She'd begun to wonder if he would do it when she felt his weight shift into her arms. Without her instructing him to do so, he twisted so they were face-to-face. His legs wrapped around her waist, easing the strain on her arms.

"Pull us up, Remington!" she shouted.

An eternity later, her gaze moved from the rocky face of the bluff to the flat surface of the plateau. She saw Remington as he led Sundown away from the ridge, and no sight had ever looked more wonderful to her.

"We're here, Sawyer," she whispered, giving the boy a little push to heft him onto the ground. A moment later she lay beside him, hugging him to her, this time in relief. "Don't you ever frighten me like that again, Sawyer Deevers. You understand me?"

"I won't."

She freed her iron grip on him and sat up. Remington joined them and knelt on the ground nearby.

"You all right, Sawyer?"

The boy nodded.

Remington turned his gaze on Libby. "You?"

"I'm fine."

Then he pulled them both into his embrace, whispering, "Thank God." He kissed Libby on the cheek, then grinned at Sawyer, and said, "Let's go home."

Nineteen

"ANNA!" NORTHROP BELLOWED AS HE stared at the telegram in his hand. He stormed out of his office, striding quickly to the sitting room. He found his wife with her needlework in hand. "When did this come?"

Her eyes widened. "What is it, Northrop?"

"Don't play innocent with me, Anna. You know good and well what it is. It's a telegram from Mr. Walker, and it was buried beneath other papers on my desk. Papers I placed there days ago."

Her voice softened to a whisper. "I'm sorry, Northrop. Perhaps it arrived while I was in the rose garden."

His eyes narrowed. There was a time when he knew when she hid the truth from him. But lately ...

"Women!" he muttered, thinking not just of Anna but also of Ellen and Olivia.

He folded the telegram in half, then folded it again as he turned his back on her. She wouldn't beat him at this game. Anna was mistaken if she thought she could best him.

And so was Olivia.

His daughter would return to this house, and she would do her duty. Her disobedience had cost him a small fortune in fees to incompetent detectives. It cost him the railroad he coveted. Worse yet, it made him the laughingstock of his peers, although they were wise enough never to let him see their amusement.

He swung around to face his wife. "I *will* be obeyed."

Anna shrank back in her chair, as if fearing he would strike her. But he preferred more enjoyable ways of torturing Anna.

He took a few steps toward her and waved the folded telegram in her face. "Don't fool yourself. I will find Olivia, and she'll be sorry she defied me." He shoved the paper into his pocket.

Anna's cheeks lost all color. "Let her go, Northrop. You have your railroad now. You don't need her to — "

"Do you think you know what I need?" Two more steps carried him to her chair. He reached down and pulled her to her feet, gripping her by the upper arms. "Do you think you can tell me what to do?"

"Northrop." She looked straight into his eyes, with a resolve he'd not seen in her before. She did not try to pull away, but kept her shoulders square, her voice calm but firm. "Let go. You're hurting me."

Her demeanor took him aback. Surprising even himself, he released his hold on her arms.

She stepped away from him immediately. "Good night, Northrop." With calm elegance, she picked up her embroidery basket and left the room.

He could have forced her to stay. He could have beaten her into submission. But instead he returned to his office where he intended to consume a great deal of brandy while contemplating his next course of action.

Remington, Libby, and Sawyer set out for the sheep camp early in the morning, a few days after Sawyer's fall. Pete Fisher had agreed to keep an eye on the place while they were gone, milking Melly and feeding the dogs and other livestock.

They rode hard, leading packhorses loaded with supplies for the herders. Remington insisted his leg was well enough to withstand the ride, but by late afternoon, Libby could see the discomfort etched in his face. She knew he would never suggest stopping for the night. He would want to continue, hoping to reach the camp before nightfall. But Libby doubted they would. It had been nearly a month since her last trip up here, and the flock would have pushed farther north and east by this time.

Libby reined Lightning to a halt. "I think we'd better stop for the night."

"How much farther is it?" Remington asked as he drew up beside her.

"At least another five hours. We can't make it before nightfall, and I don't want to attempt to find McGregor after dark, not even with a full moon."

Remington's gaze swept the area. Then he pointed to a spot not far off the trail that was sheltered by an outcropping of rocks on one side. "That looks like a good place to make camp."

With a nod, Libby nudged her gelding forward, leading the way up the gentle slope of hillside to the chosen campsite. She dismounted as soon as she reached the level area, which offered a vista of the valley below. With easy, practiced motions, she unsaddled Lightning.

Out of the corner of her eye, she noticed the way Remington favored his leg as he stepped down from the saddle. He grimaced as he rubbed his thigh.

She shouldn't have let him come. That thought caused her to smile. She could imagine the argument that would have started. If she'd learned nothing else about Remington, she'd learned he was a determined man. He didn't order or command, but neither was he easily sidetracked from his goals. She supposed that was one of the things she loved about him.

As she pulled two cans of beans from the saddlebag, she allowed her thoughts to drift back over the past six weeks. Did love happen like this for everyone? Did it take them by surprise, maybe even against their will? Did it swallow them up, consume them, make them forget everything else?

That's what it was like for her. It was a glorious discovery, a miracle, that she could feel this way. When she refused to marry a man she didn't — and couldn't — love, she hadn't known that the emotion could feel like this. More than ever, she was glad she'd refused to settle for less.

She glanced across the camp and watched Remington and Sawyer hobble the horses and turn them out to graze.

Perhaps one day she would be able to tell Remington everything. Perhaps one day she would be able to tell him about her father and mother, about a girl named Olivia Vanderhoff, about how Remington had renewed her faith in love and trust.

Perhaps one day, but not now. She didn't want to spoil the present with old heartaches.

Later that night, with a full moon rising over the eastern mountains and the heavens scattered with winking stars, Remington lay on the ground with an arm behind his head, staring upward. Long ago, when he was about seven years old, he and his father had camped out under the stars. Jefferson Walker had been home from the war about two months. The night air was filled with the sweet smell of jasmine and the sounds of bullfrogs. He remembered the honey cake Naomi, their cook, had baked for him and the musty smell of the tent his father had pitched.

Why did you give up, Father? Why didn't you keep trusting in God?

He turned his head. Across the fire from him, Libby slept on her side, her knees drawn up toward her chest. Soft moonlight caressed her face, turning her pale hair silver, erasing the freckles on her nose and the worry that so often filled her eyes. Wisps free of her braid curled about her ears and face.

I love you, Libby Blue.

As if hearing his thoughts, Libby opened her eyes. A gentle smile bowed her mouth. "Did you say something, Mr. Walker?"

"You're beautiful in the moonlight, Miss Blue."

"I've never cared if anyone thought me beautiful. Not until I met you." She let out a soft breath, almost a sigh but not quite. "You've taken away so many of my fears, Remington. I will love you forever, if only for that alone."

He longed to rise from the ground and go to her. He longed to take her in his arms and kiss her until they were both dizzy. But he stayed on his blanket. "You don't have to be afraid of anything, Libby. Not ever again. I promise."

He swore to himself that this was one promise he would never break.

Twenty

REMINGTON LIKED ALISTAIR MCGREGOR FROM the moment they first shook hands. Short of stature and wiry, McGregor had a tanned face, weathered by years in the elements, thinning dark hair streaked with gray, and an ironlike grip. His gaze was direct, unwavering.

"So ye're still here, Mr. Walker. I thought ye'd be gone when yer leg was mended." The sheep herder sounded like a suspicious father.

"No, I plan to stay."

"Is that so? And why is that, if I might ask?"

Remington glanced at Libby, then back at McGregor. "I've asked Miss Blue to marry me."

McGregor's expression didn't change in the least as he turned toward Libby. "And ye've said aye, lass?"

She nodded.

"Would ye mind tellin' me why?"

"Because, McGregor, I love him."

"Ye think him a good man?"

"I do."

The smile curving the sheep herder's mouth was infinitesimal. "Then I'm glad for ye. 'Tis a celebration we'll have tonight. Can ye tell me when the blessed union is t'take place?"

Remington put his arm around Libby's shoulders. "I've got business to settle back east, but I hope it won't take me more than a few weeks. Then I'll be on the next train headed west. We'll marry upon my return."

"I've longed t'see this lass happy, and it seems ye are makin' her so. Come an' rest a moment an' tell me all about yerself, Mr. Walker."

For the next few minutes, Remington told the Scot what he could, then ended by saying, "I'm open to suggestions on what I can do to be of help to Libby. How can we keep the Blue Springs the best sheep ranch in the territory?"

"Ye could stop that thievin' coward Bevins, for starters." McGregor grinned as he looked at Libby. "But 'tis not the time for such talk now. Ronald will be wantin' t'hear yer news, lass. He willna forgive us if we tarry any longer."

Ce

The proprietress of the Pine Station general store took only a quick glance at the photograph before handing it back to Gil O'Reilly. "Yes, I've seen him. He was here in my store not more than a week ago. Stood right there where you're standing now." She lifted her chin, her expression disapproving. "I wouldn't be at all surprised to learn Mr. Walker's in trouble with the law. Is that why you're here?"

"No, madam, 'tis not. Mr. Walker is a friend of mine." O'Reilly offered a friendly smile. "Would it be too much trouble t'ask where I might find him?"

"He's at the Blue Springs Ranch. Goodness only knows what he's doing there." She clucked her tongue. "And her with that boy living under her roof, too. It's disgraceful. Positively disgraceful. That's what it is."

Since Mrs. Jonas seemed in the mood to talk, O'Reilly would let her.

"Shameful." She shook her head. "Libby Blue should have sold that ranch after her aunt died. It's not proper for a young, unmarried woman to be living out there without another woman present, not with men in her employ. Not that there's as many men working for her these days." The woman pursed her lips as if she'd sucked on a lemon. "She doesn't fool me that Mr. Walker is working for her, either. I've been told he's livin' in the house. Livin' right in that house with her."

O'Reilly shook his head and made sympathetic sounds in his throat.

"Well." The woman drew herself up stiff as a board. "You can surely see why I don't think much of your friend."

"That I can, madam, and I'll see what I can do t'spirit him away from this Jezebel's clutches." Again he gave her a smile. "Now, if you'll be good enough t'tell me how t'find this ranch, I'll be on my way."

A few minutes later, O'Reilly walked out of the general store with a lightness in his step. If his instincts were right — and they usually were — he'd not only found Remington Walker, he'd found Vanderhoff's missing daughter.

But Remington had found her first. So why hadn't he sent word to Vanderhoff? From all O'Reilly could ascertain, Remington had been in the area for nigh onto two months.

Maybe he was wrong. Maybe this woman, this Libby Blue, wasn't the Vanderhoff girl.

O'Reilly stepped into the small black buggy he'd rented in Boise City. Once settled on the seat, he picked up the reins and clucked to the horse, starting down the road in the direction of the Blue Springs Ranch.

Remington frowned as he listened to McGregor. Would he get enough money from the sale of his home in New York and his other assets to pay back the Vanderhoff advance *and* put the Blue Springs on firm footing?

"Teddy!" Libby shouted, drawing Remington's attention.

She stood on the opposite side of the meadow where the sheep grazed. Her hat hung against her back from its leather string around her neck. She whistled and motioned with an outstretched arm. Teddy, a black-and-white collie, raced up the hillside after several ewes. The dog darted back and forth, keeping the sheep together, pushing just enough to move them down the hillside, but not so much he caused them to bolt, his actions precise and lightning quick.

When the ewes rejoined the flock, Remington's gaze returned to Libby. He heard her words of praise to the sheepdog, but it was Libby who earned his admiration.

It couldn't have been easy for her, these past years. She was raised in ease and opulence. One of her ball gowns would have paid a sheepherder's salary for an entire year, if not two. Despite adversity and hardship, she had molded herself into the woman he saw before him — capable, independent, determined.

What would Northrop think of his daughter now?

The thought made him grin. He'd grown so used to seeing Libby in trousers and boots, her hair in a braid, a wide-brimmed hat flopping against her back, that he thought nothing of it. Northrop Vanderhoff and all the Knickerbockers would be shocked. Idiots! She was exquisite just as she was. Remington would love her until his dying day. Of that there was no question.

As if she'd read his thoughts, Libby looked up, her gaze catching his from across the meadow. She smiled, and even across the distance that separated them, he saw the trust and love in her eyes. He prayed he was worthy of it.

Pete Fisher sat astride his draft horse. The animal's pace was plodding at best, and Pete's mind wandered aimlessly, as if keeping time with the horse's gait.

He was tired after a long day in the fields. All that was left was to milk Libby's cow, check the sheep in the paddock, and feed the dog and her pups. Then he could go home, sit down to supper, and call it a day. Of course, tomorrow morning, before dawn, he would be riding back to the Blue Springs to repeat the chores, but he didn't really mind. He owed a lot to Libby Blue—and to her aunt before her. Without the water from the springs, the Fishers wouldn't have a farm to work. If Bevins ever got hold of Libby's ranch, the creek would dry up quicker than a keg of cider at a barn raising.

After meeting Remington Walker, Pete figured he needn't worry about Bevins. Remington seemed the sort of man who rarely failed in what he set out to do. Bevins wouldn't be able to make any more trouble at the Blue Springs, not now that Remington and Libby were getting married. Pete would bet the farm on it.

"Guess that's exactly what I'm doing. Betting the farm."

As he crested a rise, he saw the rooftops of the house and barn above the grove of trees that surrounded the Blue Springs Ranch. He also heard the muffled but persistent barking of the dog. Something was wrong.

He kneed his horse, forcing the animal into a bone-jarring trot, and rode down the hillside and into the trees. Just as he broke into the clearing, he saw a man leave the house.

"Hey!" he shouted.

The stranger looked over his shoulder, then hopped into the buggy and whipped the horse into a gallop, disappearing almost instantly around the side of the house. Pete gave chase, but it was pointless on his old horse. The intruder's buggy was already out of sight.

He returned to the yard. Misty, shut up inside the barn, was still barking. He dismounted and opened the barn door.

"Misty, quiet," he commanded, hoping the dog would recognize his voice. When she obeyed, he reached down and patted her head. "Come on. Let's see what he was up to."

Pete searched the house but found nothing out of order, beyond the broken latch on the back door. He had no way of knowing if anything was missing; that would have to wait until Libby and Remington returned.

Ce

The campfire had burned low and Remington was drifting off to sleep when the dogs began to howl and bay.

Remington, Libby, and Sawyer were on their feet in an instant. Remington and Libby reached for their rifles in unison.

The rising moon had crested the mountains in the east, spilling a soft white light over the grazing land, but Remington couldn't see anything except sheep and trees as he cautiously moved forward. Then, above the din of barking dogs and bleating sheep, he heard an unfamiliar sound that made the hairs on the back of his neck stand on end.

Libby bolted past him at a dead run before he could react.

"Wait!" he shouted, but she didn't break her stride. He took off after her, gritting his teeth against the pain in his leg.

The sheep parted before them like water breaking before the bow of a ship. He saw McGregor across the meadow, running toward Libby. Another bloodcurdling cry split the night air just as Libby came to an abrupt halt. She raised her rifle and took aim. Remington's gaze followed the direction of the weapon's barrel.

Although he'd never seen one, he knew the animal crouched over a dead ewe was a cougar. He'd read stories about the great mountain lion of the American West.

As the dogs darted toward the cougar, it swiped with its mighty paw, barely missing them. At the same time, it let loose another scream of protest.

"Teddy, get back!" Libby shouted at the most persistent of the collies, but Teddy didn't obey. Time and time again the dog rushed forward, and time and again he escaped the giant cat's claws. "Teddy, get back! You're in the way!"

Sensing Libby's anxiety for Teddy's safety, Remington raised his own rifle, closed one eye, and stared down the barrel. He waited until the collie darted forward and backed away again, and then he fired. His aim was sure. The mountain lion fell with a thud onto its side.

Teddy's barking ceased as he eased forward, sniffing suspiciously. Remington understood how the dog felt. Neither of them would relax until they had confirmed the cougar was dead. When Remington reached the mountain lion, he poked it with the barrel of his rifle, then lifted the animal's head by the scruff of its neck and let it fall back to the ground. Reassured that the danger was over, he turned around.

Libby was kneeling on the ground, hugging Teddy and another of the dogs. Her gaze fell on the sheep near Remington's left foot. The ewe's throat had been torn open, blood turning its fleece a bright red.

"Life is fragile." She rose. "Sometimes I don't think I'm strong enough for this."

He placed his finger beneath her chin and forced her to look up at him. "You're the strongest woman I know, Libby." He kissed her forehead.

Ce

On the night she shot Remington Walker, Libby had thought him a hapless eastern dude. But he was a man who could fell a mountain lion with a single shot. He was a man who showed no fear, even when in danger.

Who are you, Remington?

He could be loving, passionate, stubborn, infuriating, tender. He had a wonderful laugh and a heart-stopping smile. He was a gentleman, a businessman, a man with polish and style, yet a man completely at ease as he milked a cow, whipped up breakfast in a crude kitchen, or helped build a chicken coop.

But who was he, really?

As she stood with him between the dead mountain lion and slain ewe, Libby considered how little either of them had talked about their pasts. She knew why she kept silent, but what were his reasons? Did he have secrets of his own?

As quickly as the doubts and questions came, she pushed them away. Remington loved her, and she loved him. God had brought them together. Nothing else mattered to her.

Twenty-One

FOUR DAYS LATER, ON THE morning of their planned return to the ranch, Sawyer asked Libby to let him stay with the sheepherders for a few weeks. Since McGregor didn't mind, Libby gave her permission. Remington might have objected if he didn't intend to hire a couple of hands before leaving for New York. He didn't want Libby alone at the ranch.

Weary and dusty, Remington and Libby rode into the yard at the Blue Springs late in the day, lengthy shadows stretching before them. Remington spied Pete Fisher's big black draft horse moments before Pete walked out of the barn, milk pail in hand.

"Glad to see you back." Pete set the pail on the ground. Coming toward them, he removed his hat and wiped the sweat from his brow. "Did you have any trouble on the trail?"

"No trouble," Remington answered as he stepped down from the saddle. "What about here?"

"I'm not sure."

"What does that mean?"

"Someone broke into the house. As far as I can tell, nothin's gone. I'd take credit for runnin' the intruder off, but he was already leavin' when I got here."

"Was it Bevins?" Libby dismounted.

"No. Wasn't nobody I knew, from what I could see. He was wearin' a hat pulled kinda low, and he was gone soon as he saw me." He shrugged. "Wasn't any way I could catch him."

Remington glanced at Libby. "You'd better check inside, see if you can tell what he was after." As Libby walked away, he turned back to Pete. "Could it have been a drifter after something to eat?"

"Could have been, I suppose, but I haven't seen many drifters drivin' buggies around."

"A buggy?" That would be an odd choice of transportation for a thief or a saddle tramp.

"Yep. A buggy." Pete tugged on his hat brim. "I'm gonna head on back to my place. Lynette's probably got supper on by this time." He pointed to the pail on the ground where he'd left it. "I got the milkin' done and fed the stock. Dogs too."

"Thanks, Pete. We're grateful for your help."

"Nothin' Libby wouldn't have done for me if I needed it. Always been good neighbors, the Blues. Amanda was the salt of the earth, and Libby's a lot like her. Like I said, glad to help. Just let me know if you need me again."

"We'll do that."

Remington waited until the farmer mounted his big workhorse and rode away, then picked up the milk pail and carried it into the house. Libby stood in the kitchen, hands on her hips, a frown creasing her forehead.

"There's no evidence that anyone was here. I've checked all the valuables. Nothing's missing. And nothing seems to be gone from the pantry either." She looked at Remington. "Why would someone break in and then take nothing? Pete said he was already leaving, so he wasn't surprised or chased away before he could steal something. What could he have wanted?"

"I don't know." Remington placed a hand on her shoulder, his own gaze moving around the room. "But I don't like it."

Northrop looked down at the telegram in his hand. It was dated June 25, 1890, three days before. He'd read the message repeatedly since receiving it, each time relishing the information. Tomorrow he would be on a train bound for Idaho. Until then, he savored the sweet taste of victory.

His eyes skimmed the telegram again.

> found walker and olivia stop will await you in weiser idaho stop send instructions care of weiser hotel stop o'reilly

Northrop folded the telegram and returned it to his breast pocket. At dinner he would break the news to Anna. Then he would see if she dared defy him.

A chorus of crickets greeted the night as darkness enveloped the Blue Springs. Inside the house, Libby stood beside her bedroom window, staring in the direction of the bunkhouse, her arms crossed as she tried to ward off the eerie feeling that had lingered throughout the evening.

Someone had been in her room. Someone had gone through her things. She'd found no evidence, but she knew. Not simply because Pete Fisher saw him leaving, but because of an unsettling aura within the house, within her room. She couldn't explain what she felt. She only knew it was real — and frightening.

She hated it when Remington went out to the bunkhouse for the night. She wanted to ask him to stay in Amanda's room again. She wanted to plead with him not to leave her alone.

An uneasiness seized her heart, a dark foreboding. She remembered how this very same foreboding used to come upon her, the sense that she would soon be discovered. She remembered the urge to run, to change her identity, to conceal herself. It had been years since she'd felt it, yet it was as familiar as hunger pangs in the morning or the need to yawn when sleepy. Years ago she could run at a moment's notice. She could find a new place to hide. But she couldn't run any longer. She had Sawyer and the ranch to think about. She had Remington. No, whatever the danger, she wasn't going to run again.

She closed the window and let the curtains fall into place, then turned around. For what must have been the twentieth time, she searched the room with her gaze, trying to find some clue, something out of place, but everything was as it had been when she left days ago.

Why had he come here, the intruder? Why, if not to steal something of value, either real or sentimental? The Monet was in its proper place. The few remaining coins in the earthenware jar hadn't been taken. Nothing was amiss in her bureau drawers.

It was as if he'd never been there.

But she felt his presence still, and she was afraid of what it meant.

Ce

Standing against the wall of the bunkhouse, Remington watched as Libby shut her bedroom window and closed the curtains, hiding her from view. He let out his breath, not realizing until that moment that he'd been holding it.

It had taken all his resolve to leave the house. He knew she wanted him to stay with her. He was glad she hadn't asked. He wasn't sure he'd have been able to deny her.

Maybe he should forget going back to New York. Maybe he should just keep Northrop Vanderhoff's money. Maybe he should hire someone back east to sell his home and divest him of his business concerns. Maybe he should marry Libby now.

His gaze moved over the moonswept landscape, looking for any sort of movement that would indicate something amiss.

What difference would it make if he didn't go back to New York?

Perhaps none. Yet he needed to be clean of Northrop's money. He didn't want to owe Northrop anything when he took Libby for his bride.

His gaze searched the black shadows that were the trees surrounding the house and yard. He couldn't make out a thing in their inky midst. Anyone could be out there, even now.

A wave of uneasiness swept through him.

Someone had been at the Blue Springs while they were gone. Someone had broken into the house. Why? What had he been after? And who was he? The most likely suspect was Timothy Bevins, even though Pete had said it wasn't. He hoped Pete was wrong about that. He hoped Bevins was behind the break-in, because if he wasn't . . .

Remington set his mouth in determination and looked at the house again. A light still burned in Libby's room, and he wondered if she was as sleepless as he. Then he sank onto the bench near the bunkhouse door, resting his rifle on his thighs, prepared to watch through the night.

Anna's eyelids felt like sandpaper. After Northrop left her bedroom, wearing that ugly, triumphant smile of his, she had wept until her tears were used up.

He'd found Olivia, and tomorrow he would go for her. He would go bring her back, drag her back in chains if he had to.

For several weeks, Anna had been able to imagine she too could break free of Northrop. Her daughter's escape had given her hope. But hope for what? She had spent her life seeing to Northrop's every need, responding to his every whim. Being the proper, obedient wife of Northrop Vanderhoff was all she knew how to do.

She knelt on the floor and reached beneath the bed, drawing out a large box. She removed the lid and stared at the yellow gown, still wrapped in tissue paper. For a brief time, she'd believed she could wear the dress. For a brief time, she'd believed she could defy Northrop.

She felt like crying again, but there were no more tears. She was dried up, like a well in a drought. She was dried up and about to blow away in a wind.

Anna leaned down until her face was hidden in the folds of the yellow dress. "Run, Olivia. Please run." Her voice fell to a whisper. "God, help her."

But faith was buried beneath despair, and she couldn't find the strength tonight to believe her prayer would be answered.

Twenty-Two

WITH A HOT SUMMER SUN burning overhead, Sundown cantered toward the Bevins spread. The three-story whitewashed house, set up against the rise of a mountain, was easy to see in the distance. No doubt Bevins watched Remington's approach.

The valley that cradled the Bevins ranch was long and wide, with thickly forested mountains forming the borders. Blue Creek cut a winding swath through the center of the valley floor. Brown-and-white cattle grazed peacefully in the tall yellow-green grass.

As Remington drew near the outbuildings, Bevins stepped onto the wide veranda that bordered two sides of the house. Remington reined Sundown to a walk, guiding the horse up close to the covered porch. He didn't dismount after stopping. Instead he tipped his hat slightly back on his head so Bevins could see his eyes. He wanted to make sure the man understood what Remington was about to tell him.

Bevins spoke first. "I'm surprised to see you here, Walker."

"I thought it was about time I paid you a visit." Out of the corner of his eye, he saw a couple of men step out of the barn and lean against the corral fence, watching and listening. "I wanted to ask your help."

"My help?" Bevins was clearly surprised.

"Yes. You know Miss Blue's been having a rough time of it this past year, but lately she seems to have had more than her share of trouble."

Bevins's face grew dark. "What's that got to do with me?"

"Nothing" — Remington leaned on his saddle horn — "I hope." He paused a couple of heartbeats. "I just thought you might keep an eye out for strangers, vagrants. You know the type. Troublemakers."

"You're takin' a mighty personal interest in that ranch of Miss Blue's."

"That's because it's about to become my ranch. Miss Blue and I are getting married." Any pretense at polite conversation disappeared from his voice. "As her husband, I mean to protect both her and what's ours. I'm not going to stand for any more sheep disappearing. There won't be any sheds burning down in the middle of the night. There won't be any runaway horses on the Pine Station road. No one's going to spread lies about my wife. Whoever's behind the trouble she's had in the past had best stop, or answer to me."

Bevins's hands closed into fists, and his face grew red with anger. "What're you accusin' me of, Walker?"

Remington raised an eyebrow, feigning innocence. "I'm not accusing you of anything, Bevins. Just passing along some information to a neighbor."

"Yeah, well, you can pass it along to someone else. It don't mean anything to me."

Remington straightened in the saddle. "I guess it's time I got back to the Blue Springs, anyway. There's plenty of work to do. Too much for one man, as a matter of fact. That's why I went down to Weiser last week and hired on some extra ranch hands. They'll be helping me keep a close eye on the place." He backed Sundown away from the porch, then tugged his hat brim, shading his eyes once more. "Good day, Bevins."

He touched his spurs to Sundown's sides and loped away.

Libby stood outside the front door and watched as the hired hands felled another tree in the grove. The tall lodgepole pine fell to the ground with a great deal of cracking and splintering and a jarring thump at the end. A cloud of dirt rose from the dry earth, briefly obscuring the men.

Remington was right about thinning the trees for a better view of the surrounding valley, but it still hurt to watch them fall. The grove of aspens, cottonwoods, lodgepoles, and tamaracks made her feel more protected than endangered. They had been her shelter from the world when she'd first come to the Blue Springs.

The sounds of axes biting into more wood filled the air. With a sigh, Libby turned and reentered the house, not wanting to watch another tree fall. She made her way to the kitchen to begin preparations for supper. The new ranch hands would be hungry after putting in such a hard day. And she wanted to prepare something special for Remington. This might well be his last night at the Blue Springs for several weeks.

He hadn't actually said he was leaving tomorrow, but she suspected it. He'd talked with McGregor, obtained the sheepherder's advice. Remington had hired more men, both to work around the ranch and, she knew, to keep an eye out for trouble while he was gone. And now he'd paid his visit to Bevins.

Her hands stilled in midair as a shiver ran up her spine. She'd dreamed of Bevins last night. She dreamed he grabbed hold of her arm and wouldn't let her pull away. He told her she'd lost, that everything was his. His fingers pinched the flesh on her arms, and he laughed as she tried to pull free. "You can't escape me," he said. "You can't get away."

And then the face and the laughter had changed, and she found herself looking into the face of her father. "You can't escape me," he repeated. "You can't get away."

She closed her eyes and leaned against the worktable, trying to drive the image from her mind. It was a silly dream. Bevins couldn't hurt her, and her father couldn't find her.

Outside, another tree came crashing down, and Libby felt a second shiver of fear, the cause of it nameless, faceless, and therefore, all the more potent.

Northrop settled back in the plush, velvet-covered chair of the Vanderhoff car, listening to the now familiar *clackety-clackety-clackety* of wheels upon rails. The sound satisfied him, perhaps because he knew where the tracks were taking him.

If the train kept on schedule, he would be in Weiser by nightfall. Tomorrow he would confront his daughter. Olivia would be surprised when she saw him, but only a little. She had to know he'd been searching for her. She had to have feared the day of discovery, even from the moment she bolted.

She couldn't have forgotten that her father was never bested, not in his business affairs or in his personal ones.

He struck a match and lit his cigar, holding it between his thumb and forefinger as he drew on it.

By Jove! He loved winning.

He exhaled a long breath of bluish gray air, watching the smoke curl in thin wisps as it rose toward the ceiling of the railcar. Then he frowned, his thoughts turning to Remington Walker, the detective he'd hired over ten months before. He wondered again why Walker had failed to report finding Olivia. Had he thought to hold out for more money? If so, he was about to regret it.

"Let her go, Northrop."

His frown deepened as he remembered Anna's plea. Only it wasn't her words that angered him. It was the spark of rebellion in her eyes.

Let Olivia go? Not like this. She'd go where he told her to go. He *would* be obeyed.

His frown turned to a smug grin.

He had taught Anna a new lesson in obedience before leaving New York City. He expected it was a lesson his wife wouldn't soon forget.

Cee

A night breeze moved softly amid the treetops. A branch from a tall pine swept its needles back and forth against a windowpane. The house creaked, then was silent; creaked, then was silent. A log in the stove shifted and crumbled, stirring new flames, and the sound filled the kitchen like a *boom*.

Libby looked across the table at Remington, feeling that same, unshakable fear squeezing her chest. "Tomorrow?"

"The sooner I go, the sooner I get back." He took hold of her right hand and held it between both of his.

She swallowed the lump in her throat. "I know. It's just that . . ." *It's just that I'm not ready for you to go yet.*

"I'll return as soon as I can. It shouldn't take long for me to take care of my business affairs. A few weeks at most."

I'm afraid, Remington. Stay with me.

Still holding her hand, he rose from his chair and came around the table, drawing Libby up to stand before him. With his free hand, he caressed the side of her face. Then he kissed her, and she tasted her own longing on his lips.

When the kiss was broken, Libby pressed her cheek against his chest. "How shall I bear it when you're gone?"

His reply was simply to tighten his arms around her.

Again she heard tree branches brushing against a window, heard the creaking of the house, heard the sizzle of the fire in the stove. All familiar sounds, but lonely. So terribly lonely.

Stay with me, she wanted to plead, but she knew she couldn't. She knew he had to go. She knew she had to let him go.

"I'd better get some sleep." He tipped her head with his index finger and planted one more kiss on her mouth. "I'll leave at first light."

"At first light." Her heart ached.

Remington drew away, and she found herself staring hard at his face, memorizing the cut of his jaw, the slight cleft in his chin, the shape of his dark brows, the midnight-blue shadows in his inky black hair. She could not rid herself of the terrible fear that she would never see him again, that he would go away and not return. She wanted to remember everything about him in case memories were all she would have left.

He touched her cheek with his fingertips one more time, then turned and left the house, closing the door softly behind him.

Stay with me!

She put out the lamp burning in the center of the kitchen table, then turned and walked through the darkened house to her bedroom.

He loves you. He'll be back. He wants to marry you. There's no reason to be afraid.

No, there wasn't any reason to be afraid, yet fear latched hold of her heart and refused to let go. The feeling had not left her since she learned someone had been in her house, had gone through her things. She couldn't shake it, no matter how often she prayed for God to remove the fear and replace it with faith.

She opened the door and stepped inside her bedroom. A gentle breeze rippled the curtains at the window, and a sheen of moonlight lightened the shadows. As she walked across the room, she tugged her shirt free from the waist of her trousers, then freed the buttons at the neck.

He'll come back. There's nothing to fear. Remington's going to return.

She sat on the edge of the bed and pulled off her boots and socks.

What if he returned to Sunnyvale and found he couldn't leave it? What if he found it was too difficult to give up his plantation and the life he'd always known?

Would he have taken me with him if I'd asked?

She closed her eyes a moment. It didn't matter if he would have taken her. She couldn't go. She couldn't leave the Blue Springs.

With a sound of frustration, she reached for her night-gown, but before her fingers touched the fabric, a hand covered her mouth. She was jerked backward so suddenly that there was no chance to scream, no chance to realize what was happening before another arm gripped her around the waist, pulling her tight against a rock-hard chest.

"Evenin', Miss Blue."

Bevins!

"Surprised to find me here, I reckon."

How had he gotten into her room? How had he gotten into the house unseen?

As if he'd heard her thoughts, he answered, "One o' them new hired hand's gonna have a lump on his head for a few days." His fingers pressed tightly against her mouth. "And if you give me trouble, you're gonna have the same. You hear me?"

She nodded, her heart pounding, her breathing rapid.

Bevins forced her to her knees, then with surprisingly deft movements replaced the hand over her mouth with a gag. The taste of the fabric was foul, and she tried to force it out with her tongue, making noises of objection.

"Quiet."

He jerked her arms behind her back and tied her wrists together. The rope pinched her skin, making her eyes water.

Again she protested, trying her best to scream through the gag. This time he cuffed her into silence. The blow knocked her onto her side on the floor and left her ears ringing.

Bevins leaned over her. "Don't cause me no trouble, and maybe you won't suffer."

She'd underestimated him. She'd thought him a troublemaker and a thief but a coward. She hadn't suspected . . . this.

"Walker thought he'd scare me off. He thought he could tell me to keep away from you and this ranch. Well, you're not gonna marry him. This ranch is gonna be mine, and I'm not waitin' any longer to get it."

In the pale moonlight, she saw the madness in his eyes. Her blood turned to ice in her veins. He meant what he'd said. He would kill her.

"Shame this house has gotta go. I might've been able to use it. 'Course, it's not as big as mine, but there's plenty of nice things here. Too bad I can't save 'em."

She tried to rise, but he pushed her back onto her side with his foot.

"Fire's gotta start where you are." Bevins looked around. "Otherwise they might get you out in time. This room's no good. Lover boy might see through the window."

Fire? God, help me.

"Guess I could put you on the sofa. Have the fire start out there. Yeah, I think that's what I better do. Start the fire where it won't be seen so soon."

Remington!

Twenty-Three

REMINGTON LAY ON HIS BUNK, staring at the ceiling, waiting for sleep. Across the room, Jimmy Collins snored softly. Remington supposed he should be thankful. Fred Miller sounded like a grizzly bear when he slept, his snores all but shaking the rafters of the bunkhouse. But Fred had the first watch tonight, and with any luck, Remington would be asleep before Fred came in to trade places with Jimmy.

Except Remington knew he wouldn't sleep, no matter how silent the room. Whether his eyes were open or closed, he envisioned the way Libby had looked at him tonight, trying to be brave yet unable to hide her sadness, her uncertainty. He kept hearing her whisper, *"How shall I bear it when you're gone?"*

How will I bear it?

He wouldn't be away long. Only a few weeks.

How will I bear it?

He sat up, lowering his feet over the side of the bed; then, with elbows resting on his thighs, he cradled his head in his hands. His deceit lay like a stone on his heart.

He understood why Libby concealed her identity. He no longer considered it a lie. She *was* Libby Blue. He, on the other hand, had used his given name but lied about everything else.

"God, I've made a mess of things. How do I unravel it all?"

Go to Libby. The words seemed to fill the room. *Go now.*

In response, Remington shot to his feet, like a soldier obeying an order. *I've got to tell her the truth.* He reached for his trousers.

He didn't know if God had spoken to him in answer to his pitiful cry for help, or if it was his own conscience talking. Whichever it was, he meant to tell Libby the truth. All of it.

He pulled on his shirt.

She wouldn't hate him. She loved him and would forgive him once he explained everything.

Swift strides carried him across the yard to the back door. He entered the kitchen and stepped toward the table with the intention of lighting the lamp. As he reached for it, a sound stopped him. A sound so soft he shouldn't have heard it. A sound out of place in this house, in the night.

All his senses went on alert. He eased back from the table, peering down the dark hallway toward Libby's room, listening, waiting. Then he heard it again. A moan. A sigh. He couldn't be certain which.

The door to Libby's room flew open, and Remington withdrew into the kitchen. Then he heard a deep voice mutter a curse.

Bevins. Bevins was with Libby.

Remington clenched and unclenched his hands, concentrating on each sound, each shifting shadow.

"Get out there," he heard Bevins order. "On the sofa."

Libby lunged out of the bedroom, as if pushed. He heard her muffled protest and knew she was gagged.

He controlled his white-hot fury, biding his time, waiting for the right moment. He couldn't afford a mistake, not with Libby's life in the balance. Not after she'd touched his heart and changed him. Not after she'd shown him that love was more important than revenge. Not after she'd helped him find his way back to the faith his father taught him as a boy.

The shadow that was Bevins followed Libby into the living room. Remington inched his way down the hall. He needed his revolver, but he couldn't go for it now. He didn't even dare look for Libby's shotgun. Surprise was his best weapon.

He paused at the corner, listening once again. Logs were being tossed onto the grate as Bevins muttered to himself. Remington eased forward to peer into the parlor.

Libby was on the sofa. Bevins crouched at the fireplace, his back to the entry. The time to act was now.

God, make my leg strong.

With that prayer, Remington hurled himself at the hunched figure.

Libby heard Bevins grunt and opened her eyes. She saw the darkened shapes of the two men as they rolled on the floor. Bevins shouted a vile curse as the fire tongs clattered onto the hearth.

Remington!

Knuckles hit flesh. A sharp intake of breath. Another grunt.

"Libby, get out of here! Run!"

She pushed off the sofa, struggling against the rope that bound her wrists as she rushed for the doorway.

"Oomph!"

She turned at the sound, knowing it was Remington who'd made it, wondering if he was hurt. But she couldn't help him this way. She turned again and ran down the hall into the kitchen. With her back to the door, she fumbled with the knob, trying to open it. Above the pounding of her heart, she heard something in the living room crash to the floor and shatter. More swearing, more groans.

She fumbled with the doorknob. *Please. Oh, please open.*

Tears of frustration pooled in her eyes as her fingers slipped away again and again. She had to get to the bunkhouse. She had to get help for Remington.

It was useless. Her hands were bound too tightly. She couldn't grip the knob. She couldn't open the door.

A knife. Perhaps she could cut the rope and —

The sudden silence seemed louder than the fighting had been. She pressed her back against the door, waiting.

God, let him be all right.

She heard the strike of the match, saw a pale flicker of light at the end of the hall. The light brightened as a lamp's wick caught flame.

She couldn't breathe. She couldn't move.

Remington, please be okay.

He stepped into view, lamp in hand.

A choked sob escaped her. She pushed away from the door, stumbling, nearly falling. And then he was there, holding her in his arms, murmuring her name as he freed her wrists and removed the foul gag from her mouth.

"You're all right," she whispered. "You're all right."

"I'm all right." Remington cradled her face with his hands and stared into her eyes. "What about you? Did he hurt you?"

She shook her head. "No. No, he didn't hurt me." She touched a cut on the corner of his mouth, then brushed his hair back from his forehead. His left eye would be bruised and swollen tomorrow. She saw signs of it already. But he was all right. He was alive. That was all that mattered.

He gave her another tight hug. "You'd better sit down."

Libby obeyed, her legs too wobbly to support her another moment.

"I'll be right back." Remington walked to the living room, disappearing from view.

Bevins had planned to burn down the house with her in it. He'd planned to murder her. The horror of it returned tenfold. She clutched her abdomen as the shaking spread through her, making her weak, leaving her sick.

She heard footsteps and looked up. Terror blazed in her chest at the sight of Bevins walking toward her. Then she realized Bevins's arms were behind his back, as if tied, and that Remington was right behind him. Bevins's face was bloodied and bruised.

"Stop," Remington ordered when they reached the table. Then he lit a second lamp and picked it up. "Wait here, Libby. I won't be long."

Remington took Bevins to a storage room in the barn. Once there, he bound his prisoner's ankles and wrists with more rope.

"You can wait here for the sheriff." Remington forced Bevins to sit on the dusty board floor. "Consider yourself lucky that I don't hang you myself."

With one eye on Bevins, he cleared the storage room of tack, tools, hoes, and shovels. He left nothing that could be used to cut the ropes, nothing the man could use as a weapon if he got loose. Then, taking the lamp with him, Remington closed and secured the door.

He was impatient to return to Libby, but first he had to find out what happened to Fred Miller. He awakened Jimmy Collins and sent him to the barn to guard Bevins. A few minutes later, Remington located Fred on the edge of the old grove. The ranch hand was just regaining consciousness as Remington knelt beside him.

Fred tenderly touched the back of his head as he sat up. "I'd like t'get my hands on whoever done this."

"He's trussed up in the barn now." Remington told Fred what had happened, then offered to help him back to the bunkhouse.

"I'm okay, boss. I can make it to there on my own. You go see about Miss Blue."

Remington was only too happy to comply.

He found Libby seated where he'd left her. Her face was pale, her eyes wide with lingering fear. Even from the doorway, he saw her body shaking.

Reaching Libby, he drew her up from the chair and into his arms. She seemed to melt against him.

"It's all right," he whispered, stroking her back.

"He was going to burn down the house."

"He can't do anything now. He's tied up and locked in the storeroom in the barn."

She shook her head, her forehead touching his chest. "He was going to kill me."

"He won't be killing anybody. We'll send for the sheriff tomorrow."

She looked up at him. "I thought ... I thought ..."

"I know." He turned, still holding her with one arm. "Come on. Let's get you to bed." He took up the lamp with his other hand.

She leaned on him, letting him guide her down the hall and into her bedroom. When they reached the bed, she grabbed hold of his hand, gripping him as if her life depended on it. "Don't leave me alone, Remington." Quiet desperation filled each word, each syllable. "Please."

"I won't." He set the lamp on the nearby stand, then gently urged her to sit on the edge of the bed. "Lie down, Libby," he said softly.

"Don't go."

"I won't." He pressed her shoulders back until her head touched her pillow. "I'm going to sit in that chair by the window and keep watch all night."

"I was so afraid."

"I'm here, Libby. No one can hurt you now. You mean too much to me to let anyone harm you. I promise."

Twenty-Four

As DAWN SPILLED THROUGH THE window, Libby sat up in bed and stared across the room. As promised, Remington was still in the nearby chair, but sleep had overtaken him some time during his watch.

Libby tossed aside the blankets and sat up. She had slept in her clothes and felt rumpled and unkempt. A bath, some tooth powder, and a change of clothes would make her feel better.

A floorboard creaked under her weight. Remington shot to his feet.

"It's just me," she said as he looked around the room with sleep-filled eyes.

He groaned and rubbed the back of his neck. "That's not a very comfortable chair."

"I'm sorry. I shouldn't have asked you to stay."

He gave her a wry smile. "You couldn't have made me leave." Two long strides brought him to her. He cradled her face between his hands. "Good morning."

Libby blushed. It was silly, she supposed. She had tended his gunshot wounds when he couldn't tend to himself. They'd been together in the mornings when they were on the trail. He'd even seen her in her dressing gown and slippers the night the shed burned down. But for some reason, this was different. Perhaps because they were in her bedroom together, just the two of them, at this early hour.

Remington kissed her forehead. "Did you sleep well?"

She nodded, surprised that it was true.

He drew her closer, resting his chin atop her head. "I never would've forgiven myself if something had happened to you."

Awash with love, Libby let herself soak up the safety and warmth of his embrace.

"I love you, Libby. More than you may ever know. I hope . . . I hope you'll always believe that."

"I will," she whispered.

They stayed like that for a long while, holding one another as the glow of morning light filled the room, neither of them moving, neither speaking.

But at last Remington broke the tender spell. "I'd better go check on our prisoner and send Fred for the sheriff. The sooner that's taken care of, the better."

"I couldn't agree more." She shuddered.

"There're some things we need to talk about before I leave for New York. Things I should've told you before now."

Libby didn't want to think about him leaving. Not now. Not yet.

He kissed her cheek. "Wait for me in the kitchen. We'll talk as soon as I'm done outside."

Northrop studied the passing terrain. He hadn't seen another buggy or horseback rider or even a farmhouse since they'd left Weiser at daybreak. He couldn't fathom his daughter living in such a remote area, without even the simplest necessities to make life enjoyable.

Harder still was absorbing the additional information O'Reilly had gleaned while waiting for Northrop's arrival in Idaho. According to some woman at a place called Pine Station, Remington Walker and Olivia — or rather, Libby Blue, as she called herself — were engaged to be married.

He frowned. Walker was no fool. He couldn't possibly hope to inherit the Vanderhoff fortunes by marriage. The only plausible explanation, then, was that Walker had fallen in love with Northrop's daughter.

Love. A highly overrated emotion. Northrop had seen intelligent men do many foolish things in the name of love.

His mouth curved in a knowing smile. He hadn't built the Vanderhoff fortunes without understanding how to use basic human nature to his own advantage. If his instincts proved correct, Olivia would be more than willing to return with him to New York before this day was over.

He looked at O'Reilly. "How much longer before we reach that ranch?"

"Not long, sir. We're nearly there."

Libby whipped up a breakfast of biscuits and gravy, pork sausage, and fried eggs and set out a pitcher of chilled milk, brought up from the springs, in the center of the table. When all was ready, she rang the bell outside the back door.

Moments later, Remington and Fred entered the kitchen. Libby listened as Fred apologized for letting Bevins sneak up on him, then she made a fuss over the lump and scab on the back of his head. After the two men sat down to eat, she dished up another plate and took it out to Jimmy, who was on his second turn at guard duty.

"What about him?" Jimmy jerked his head toward the closed door of the temporary jail.

A cold chill seeped into her. "Remington will bring out food when he's through with his own breakfast." She left quickly, eager to be in the warming rays of the morning sunlight.

She had nearly reached the kitchen door when she saw a buggy approaching, her view of the road unimpeded now that many of the trees had been cleared. She raised a hand to her brows, shading her eyes as she tried to make out the visitors, but the black top of the surrey cast deep shadows over the two people on the carriage seat.

Misty ran to the edge of the yard and barked a quick warning. In a higher, sharper pitch, Ringer mimicked his mother, and the rest of the puppies followed suit. Misty looked back at her mistress, waiting for a command.

Libby stepped away from the house as the buggy drew closer, the horse traveling at a brisk trot. The driver didn't slow the animal to a walk until the carriage passed through the break in the trees.

Libby felt wary as she waited. She couldn't take her eyes off the passenger in the fine black surrey with its red carriage stripe and green cloth trimmings, watching as sunlight climbed from his chest ... to his neck ... to his face.

Her throat went dry. Her body stiffened and refused to move.

Not now.

The buggy drew to a halt in front of her, and her father descended. His steely gaze studied her for what seemed an eternity.

Not now ... not now ... not now.

"Well, Olivia, I am here at last." He lifted an iron-gray eyebrow. "Have you no greeting for me after so many years?"

Not now.

She opened her mouth to speak, but the words wouldn't come out. She remembered the dream she'd had two nights ago, heard her father saying, *"You can't escape me,"* felt her own helplessness choking her.

Then she heard the door open. Her father's gaze shifted to a place over her shoulder.

Remington's here. It will be okay.

Those simple words gave her courage. Remington was with her. She could face her father with him at her side. She could face anything as long as Remington was near. Her father had no more power over her. Not now. Not ever again.

She turned, watched Remington's approach, saw the flinty expression in his eyes, the hard set of his mouth.

"It's good to see you again, Mr. Walker," her father said.

Libby's breathing became shallow, difficult.

Remington glanced at her, tried to hold her gaze, but she turned away. She had to look at her father once again.

"I'm glad your search was successful." Northrop continued to speak to Remington. "I'm certain you are too, considering the tidy sum you've made for less than a year's work."

Father can't possibly know him. It's not true.

"Libby," Remington said softly.

"I'm sorry I wasn't able to reply to your telegram to inform you of my arrival, but I felt it would be better to surprise Olivia." He pulled a bank draft from his breast pocket. "This is the bonus we agreed upon. As you can see, I'm a man of my word. You found Olivia before your year was over." He held the draft at arm's length. "When you return to Manhattan, send round an invoice for your expenses and the remainder of your agency fee. I'll have my man at the bank issue the payment at once."

Libby took the draft from her father's hand before Remington could move. She stared at it, but the numbers blurred together. She blinked to clear her vision, then blinked again.

It was made out to Remington Walker. She read his name over and over.

Her father had known Remington was here. He'd brought the bank draft with him. He knew Remington. He knew him. He —

Remington's hand alighted on her shoulder. "Libby, listen to me."

Her eyes refocused on the amount of the draft. She read it aloud. "Two hundred and fifty thousand dollars." She shook her head, disbelieving. "A quarter of a million dollars." She glanced up. "Is that what I'm worth, Father? So very much? I didn't know. I never imagined how much you valued me."

"Libby," Remington tried again.

She turned and stared at Remington, wanting — *needing* — to see something in his expression that wasn't there. "Tell me it isn't true, Remington. Tell me Father didn't hire you to find me. Tell me."

But he didn't deny it. She saw the truth in eyes.

"I can explain, Libby."

"Explain what, young man?" Northrop interrupted in a loud, cheerful voice. He stepped forward to take hold of Libby's arm, drawing her away from Remington. "You've confirmed your reputation as the best detective in Manhattan. You've done what no one else could do, and believe me, there are plenty who've tried." Northrop turned Libby to face him, taking the bank draft from her fingers as he spoke to her again. "I can't imagine there's anything you want to take with you from this wretched place, Olivia, but if there is, get it now. We've a train to catch."

"You mean too much to me to let anyone harm you." Remington's words, only last night thought to be a declaration of love, now took on a different meaning. He'd kept her safe from Bevins so he could collect his reward from her father. It wasn't love that had motivated him. It was greed. She'd been bought and sold once again.

"Libby, I can explain."

She stared at the bank draft. "This is why you went into Weiser. To send a telegram to my father."

"Yes, but—"

"And then you asked me to marry you. Why? Why bother with more pretense?"

"It wasn't pretense. I love you." Remington stepped forward, took the bank draft from her hand, and ripped it in two. "I don't want your father's money, and I didn't tell him I found you. I couldn't do it. He's lying to you."

Northrop laughed, a sound without humor. "Do you take Olivia for a fool? Why else would I be here? I haven't known where she was all these years. If not for your telegram, I still wouldn't know. And if you thought you could get more money out of me by marrying her, you were mistaken. My lawyers would have seen to a quick annulment." He took hold of Libby's arm, drawing her gaze. "You haven't married him already, have you?"

She shook her head.

"Libby," Remington said softly. "Please listen to me. I didn't betray you. Please believe me."

I can't. Tears welled in her eyes. *I can't believe you. You lied to me. All this time, you were lying to me. Father wouldn't have found me if not for you. I was safe until you came to the Blue Springs.*

"Your father can't take you against your will."

She supposed Remington was right. He couldn't take her against her will. But what did it matter now? Everything she'd wanted, all she'd held dear, all her hopes for the future, had been shattered in minutes. And now that he'd found her, her father would destroy this ranch and the lives of all who lived here if she resisted him. She would never be free of him now. Perhaps, with Remington by her side, she could have fought her father. But Remington wouldn't be by her side. Remington had betrayed her.

Her father's hold on her arm tightened. "Your mother is anxious to see you, Olivia. Her heart's been broken by your absence. Don't make her wait any longer. Let's go."

"Mama," Libby whispered. A desperate longing to be held in her mother's arms welled in her chest, and she allowed her father to draw her toward the buggy.

"Libby, what about Sawyer?" Remington demanded.

When she hesitated, her father leaned close to her ear. "Give me no more trouble, Olivia, and I'll see that the orphan boy is well taken care of."

She'd lost. She'd lost her bid for freedom from her father's control and she'd lost her ability to protect and care for Sawyer and she'd lost her dreams of love and a happy marriage. Worse still, she'd lost hope.

Without looking behind her, she answered Remington, "Tell McGregor I'll send him the deed to the ranch. He'll take care of Sawyer." She choked back a sob as she stepped into the buggy. "Tell them I said good-bye."

"Let's go, O'Reilly," her father barked to the driver.

A blessed numbness spread icy tentacles throughout Libby's body as the buggy sped away from the Blue Springs.

Twenty-Five

September 1890
New York City

THE VAST DRAWING ROOM OF the Alexander Harrison home on Fifth Avenue was crowded and stuffy. From one end of the room to the other, the cream of New York society gossiped and pontificated, their individual conversations merging into one noisy hum of voices. Across the hall, in the music room, a small orchestra played the "Blue Danube" waltz, the sweet strains of the violins drifting above the general din.

Remington stood near the fireplace with three other men, acquaintances from his private club. Like them, he was dressed in evening attire — a white shirt with a high stiff collar and cuffs, a black bow tie, a white waistcoat with a shawl collar and two pockets, and a gold watch and chain. His jacket and trousers were the color of soot, his cotton gloves a contrasting white. And like the men around him, he was welcome in the Harrison home because he had the proper resources, breeding, and connections to make him suitable company for the unmarried women present this evening.

But Remington came to see only one woman. He waited for Libby Blue.

The story of the disappearance of Northrop's daughter had been whispered in parlors and drawing rooms for a number of years. It was no secret that the shipping magnate had hired detectives to find her, although none of this was discussed in Northrop's presence. Now everyone accepted—or pretended to accept—the trumped-up story that Olivia Vanderhoff had been selflessly nursing an ailing friend all these years.

The ability of power and wealth to alter the truth never ceased to amaze Remington. Facts and memories, even history itself, could be changed in the blink of an eye—or at the will of a man like Vanderhoff.

Charlton Bernard brought his personal take on the story of Olivia Vanderhoff to a close. "I've heard she was overcome by the death of her friend and hasn't left Rosegate since her return."

George Webster glanced toward the host and hostess on the far side of the room. "Penelope Harrison must be beside herself with joy that Miss Vanderhoff chose this soiree for her first public appearance. Mother is pea-green with envy. She'll take to her bed with a headache for the next three days."

The other men laughed. All but Remington.

"I hear Miss Vanderhoff is a real beauty," Michael Worthington commented.

As Charlton and George gave their hearty concurrence, Remington thought of Libby as she'd looked the morning he'd last seen her, over two months before. He remembered the sparkle in her green eyes, the inviting curve of her mouth, the luster of her hair, the softness of her creamy white skin.

Charlton chuckled. "You can be sure plenty of suitors will leave their cards at Rosegate after this night. Now that she's returned to good society, Miss Vanderhoff will have no lack of men seeking her hand in marriage."

Remington's fingers tightened around his glass.

"And do you plan to be one of them?" George elbowed Charlton in the ribs.

"If I want to make my parents happy, I will. Have you any idea how much Vanderhoff is worth? And his daughter is his only legitimate heir."

Remington excused himself, unable to bear the conversation another minute. What would they think if he told them the truth? What would they think if he told them Libby shot him when he found her living on a sheep ranch?

He weaved through the crowd, offering a word here and there but avoiding any lengthy exchanges. Finally he chose a spot in a corner beside a giant porcelain vase overflowing with American Beauty roses. He fixed his eyes on the doorway and waited for a glimpse of Libby, just as he'd waited outside Rosegate, hoping for a glimpse of her. He'd taken up his post daily, without success, for almost an entire month. Tonight would be different.

Half an hour later, his wait was rewarded — but not by Libby Blue.

Olivia Vanderhoff stood framed in the doorway of the drawing room. Her hair was worn high on her head, exposing the length of her slender neck. Her throat and ears sparkled with brilliant diamonds. There wasn't so much as a hint of a smile on her mouth, and her eyes seemed to stare with cool disregard, as if she didn't see the people around her. She wore an elegant gown of dusty rose — draped, pleated, and bustled.

She looked exquisite, but Remington would have preferred to see her in a flannel shirt and denim trousers. He would have preferred to see Libby.

Penelope Harrison, Alexander's second wife, had been a classmate of Olivia's at finishing school. Though never especially close, no one would have guessed, given the welcome Penelope gave her.

"Olivia, dearest! I'm so delighted you came this evening." Penelope clasped Olivia's hands, then leaned forward and kissed both of her cheeks. She turned toward the gentleman at her right. "Olivia, this is my husband, Alexander Harrison. I don't believe the two of you have been introduced. Mr. Harrison was in Europe when you ... when you went away."

Alexander, a handsome man in his midforties, bowed at the waist. "A pleasure, Miss Vanderhoff. My wife has been awaiting your arrival with great anticipation."

Olivia inclined her head ever so slightly. "Thank you, sir. It's a pleasure to make your acquaintance."

Her father stepped forward to shake Alexander's hand, apologizing for their tardiness. "My wife took suddenly ill, and we were waiting for the doctor."

"I hope it's nothing serious," Penelope said with what sounded like genuine concern.

Northrop shook his head. "No. Nothing more than a cold, I suspect. My wife suffers from a rather delicate constitution."

Olivia gritted her teeth. Her mother had neither a cold nor a delicate constitution. Northrop had forbidden his wife to come to the Harrison soiree.

"It's bad enough, Anna, that I have a daughter who looks as cheerful as a corpse," he'd shouted earlier that evening, his voice ringing through the house. *"I'll not have you dragging about as if you're in mourning. I'll make your excuses."*

Poor Mama.

Penelope slipped her arm through Olivia's. "You've been gone so very long. Let me introduce you to my guests. I'm sure your father won't mind if I steal you away."

It mattered little to Olivia whether she was stolen away from her father or whether she met any of the other guests. Nothing had mattered to her since the moment she'd stepped into that buggy and left—

With cool precision, she cut off the rest of that thought. She was all right, as long as she didn't allow herself to remember. She could survive as long as she didn't think about what had been. She'd become an expert at excising memories, at blacking them out, cutting them off before they took hold and hurt her again.

Because nothing mattered to her, she could be and do whatever her father wanted. And tonight he wanted her to come to the Harrisons' soiree.

She wondered whom her father had in mind as her prospective bridegroom among the men here. Several years ago, Gregory James had found a different heiress to wed, but surely Northrop had his eye on another lucrative arrangement, the only possible reason her father would insist she attend the party. He did nothing without reason or purpose.

"Gentlemen, look whom I've brought to you," Penelope said, drawing Olivia's attention to the present. "Olivia, you remember Mr. Bernard and Mr. Webster."

She gave them each a cool smile. Charlton Bernard's grandfather had made his fortune in real estate. It was possible, but not likely, that he was her chosen suitor. George Webster's family owned fabric mills in upstate New York. Probably not the right sort of money for her father. Northrop would prefer a son-in-law with the proper pedigree in addition to his other assets.

"And this is Michael Worthington. He moved to New York from Atlanta several years ago, and he's taken us all with his southern charm."

"A pleasure, Miss Vanderhoff." Michael took her gloved hand and kissed her knuckles. "May I offer my condolences? I understand you recently lost someone close to you."

A picture flashed in her head — rugged mountains, golden aspens, and green pines, pastures dotted with woolly sheep, black-and-white puppies tumbling in grassy fields, a log house, Sawyer, and —

She stiffened. "Thank you."

"May I also say that word of your beauty failed to prepare me for the stunning reality?"

"You're so beautiful, Libby. I love you."

Olivia swallowed, refusing to envision the man who had spoken those words.

She pulled the cold, protective shell tight around her heart. "Thank you again, Mr. Worthington."

"Behave yourself, Michael Worthington." Penelope tapped his arm with her fan. "Mr. Vanderhoff might not approve of you speaking so boldly to his daughter on your first meeting." Then, with a laugh, she drew Olivia away from the three bachelors.

Olivia moved like a doll, allowing her hand to be kissed without feeling touched, saying the proper words without hearing what was said to her, looking into people's eyes without seeing anything. She forced a smile when she knew one was expected from her. She held herself straight and regal.

She performed perfectly, just as Northrop Vanderhoff's daughter was expected to perform.

Remington watched the charade with an aching heart. He saw beneath the practiced facade, saw the brittle woman within, and knew that he was the cause of it.

I'm sorry, Libby.

He would do anything, give anything, to win her forgiveness, to earn back her love. That's what had brought him to this house tonight.

After Libby left the Blue Springs, Remington was swamped by guilt. Memories of Libby had surrounded him. In the house. In the barn. In the paddock. Up on the trail. At the summer range. Everywhere. Without her, nothing was right. Nothing made sense.

Which was why, as soon as they were able, he and Sawyer had come to New York. They'd come to get Libby, and they weren't going back to Idaho without her.

Through the crush, he saw Libby break away from Penelope Harrison and make her way toward the glass doors that led out to the courtyard. Slipping unobtrusively from his corner, he followed her, knowing that his chance had, at last, arrived.

Olivia drew in a deep breath of air, thankful to have escaped the crowd. She wasn't used to having so many people around. It had been years since she'd attended such a gathering. She'd forgotten what it was like — the noise, the heat, everyone pressed together, having no room to move with ease.

She proceeded across the stone courtyard toward a break in the tall shrubs, away from the glaring light spilling through the glass doors. But even in the garden beyond the shrubbery and courtyard, she found no peace, perhaps because it was so small. Another tall house rose to the left and another to the right and still another across the alley. She felt trapped, confined. She longed for wide vistas and sweeping valleys and —

No, don't remember.

Sinking onto a marble bench, she lifted her face. Such a tiny patch of black velvet sky. So few stars. There was a place where the sky seemed to go on for eternity. A place —

Don't remember.

She squeezed her eyes closed and let her head fall forward again. Why was she plagued with these thoughts tonight? It didn't matter anymore. None of it mattered anymore.

Better to forget. It was so much better to forget. That was the advantage of being caught in a crowd of laughing, talking people. It was more difficult to think. She should go back inside before —

"Hello, Libby."

Her breath caught.

"I've missed you."

Oh, God, have mercy on me.

"Libby?"

She turned as Remington stepped toward her. In the shadows of the tall shrubs, he was little more than a shadow himself, yet her mind saw him with clarity. She saw his devastating smile, the light in his blue eyes, the slight wave in his black hair. She saw the breadth of his shoulders, the length of his legs.

She saw his deception. She heard his lies.

Olivia rose from the bench. "I didn't know you were in New York, Mr. Walker."

"I've been here a few weeks. It took me some time to clear up the matter of Bevins with the authorities. He won't be back to bother you again, Libby. He'll be in jail until he's an old man." He took another step toward her. "I've wanted to see you ever since I arrived. I've been waiting for an opportunity to talk in private."

Like a heavy woolen cloak, she pulled indifference about her, shielding her heart. "I can't imagine we have anything more to say to each other."

She moved to step around him, but he caught hold of her arm in a gentle grasp.

"Libby . . ."

She looked into his eyes. "I'd rather you didn't call me that."

"But—"

"Leave me alone, Mr. Walker. There is nothing for either of us to say. The past is best forgotten."

"I need to tell you the truth."

"I already know the truth. Father showed me his files, the cancelled payments to you, all of your telegrams."

"Not all of them. He didn't show you the last one I sent, or you would believe me. You'd know that I — "

She pulled her arm free and moved toward the court-yard, not wanting to listen to his lies.

"Libby, Sawyer is with me. He'd like to see you."

A tiny gasp rushed through her parted lips as she turned. "You brought Sawyer to New York?"

"Yes."

Don't be a fool. You can't be anything to Sawyer now. Father would —

Remington held out his hand. "Here's my card. Sawyer is always there in the morning, with his tutor. If you won't come to see me, at least come to see him. He misses you. He loves you."

Despite her better judgment, Olivia took the card. She stared down, trying so hard not to see, not to care.

"I miss you too, Libby."

From within the house, she heard the sweet strains of a Tchaikovsky waltz begin.

"Remember the night we danced?" Remington asked, his voice low. "Dance with me again."

"No," she whispered.

"I love you, Libby."

She stepped backward as if he'd slapped her. "Mr. Walker, of all the lies you told me, that was the cruelest one of all." Then she whirled and hastened into the house.

In her wake, Remington's calling card fluttered to the ground.

Twenty-Six

REMINGTON SOMETIMES WISHED HE WERE a drinking man. He would drown all his regrets, all his guilt, all his self-recriminations, in a bottle of brandy. But his father had taught him that liquor held no answers, and the lesson stayed with him.

He turned his gaze toward the fireplace, watching flames lick at the logs on the grate.

It had been nearly a week since the Harrison party, and still Libby hadn't come to visit Sawyer. She loved the boy as if he were her own son. Remington had been certain she wouldn't be able to stay away.

He leaned against the padded back of the leather chair, closing his eyes against the grim truth: she hated him more than she loved Sawyer.

That's a lot of hate.

How could he overcome her hate if he couldn't see her, talk to her, explain things? Despite appearances, he had protected her, not betrayed her.

Still, it was his fault Northrop had found Libby. He should have done something to cover his tracks. He should have known Northrop would hire other detectives. He should have led the hired lackeys away from Libby. He should have done a lot of things differently — beginning with telling her the whole truth as soon as he knew he loved her.

He sat forward, his forearms resting on his thighs.

Sitting and thinking of the things he should have done, the things he shouldn't have done, would get him nowhere. That wasn't going to win Libby back. That wasn't going to free her of her father's stranglehold. He needed a plan.

He couldn't walk up to the Vanderhoff mansion and present his calling card. Even if Northrop allowed him to enter, Libby would refuse to talk to him. No, his best course of action was to seek her out away from Rosegate. Which meant he had to increase his social activities. Which meant he had to play the part of the marriageable bachelor. He would need to attract invitations to all the right homes and suppers and soirees and balls.

Remington rose and strode across the room to the fireplace. He leaned an arm on the mantel, staring once again into the fire.

Though his connections allowed him to move in the highest circles of New York society, he'd never cared to venture there. He had concentrated instead on increasing his personal fortunes. He mingled with the right men on Wall Street, and with their help, he invested wisely. On occasion he dined at their homes and met their wives and their daughters, but he never showed interest in matrimony. He had but one goal since his father died: find a way to destroy Northrop Vanderhoff.

He struck the mantel with his fist. What a fool he'd been! What a blind, ignorant fool!

"I'm not going to give up, Libby. I'm not ever going to give up."

The supper party at Rosegate was a small affair — a select thirty guests, many of them descendants of the original Knickerbocker families, the nucleus of Manhattan society since the beginning of the century. There were a few exceptions, most notably the guest of honor, the Honorable Spencer Lambert, Viscount Chelsea, heir to the tenth Earl of Northcliffe.

The viscount, seated on Olivia's left, had been attentive to her throughout the first ten courses. He sought to entertain her with stories of his adventures in the American West, bemoaning his failure to encounter an American bison but pleased about both the grizzly bear and the elk he'd managed to bring down.

Spencer was the man her father had selected to be her husband. Olivia knew it even though nothing had been said to her. She wondered if the viscount would care that she could never love him and would likely despise him. But then, perhaps an English lord in need of a fortune to bolster his coffers didn't care about such trivialities.

"I must tell you, Lord Lambert," Penelope Harrison chimed in from across the table, "we are delighted you returned to Manhattan."

"So am I," he replied, his gaze on Olivia. "Indeed, so am I."

She tried to make herself smile, but it was a halfhearted attempt. What she did or said mattered little. She wasn't required to charm the viscount. The dowry her father offered would do that for her.

Olivia looked down the length of the table. Her father sat at the head, his face mostly obscured by glittering candelabra.

How much would he pay to marry her off to this Englishman? He had spent a great deal to find her and bring her back. How much more would he spend to send her away?

It was rumored that Anson Stager put up a million dollars for his daughter, Ellen, to become the Lady Arthur Butler. Lily Hammersley was now the Duchess of Marlborough, at the price of four million dollars. The former Anita Murphy joined the ranks of American heiresses in England for two million dollars.

How much for me, Father?

She turned her attention back to Spencer, looking at him with a cool, detached eye. He was handsome enough, she supposed, with his golden hair and pale brown eyes. His face was narrow and clean-shaven. He was a few years older than she, perhaps not yet thirty.

He would want an heir. Besides money to replenish drained accounts, that's what these marriages were about, really, begetting a son to carry on the title.

Unexpectedly she thought of a boy with tousled coffee-colored hair and dark brown eyes full of mischief, and her heart ached. Sawyer was in Manhattan. She remembered the Madison Avenue address of Remington's home as if it had been engraved on her mind instead of on his card.

It must have hurt Sawyer, her leaving the way she had, without so much as a good-bye. He'd lost both his parents. He wouldn't understand why she had abandoned him.

If she could go to him . . . If she could try to explain why she'd had to leave . . . If she could let him know she loved him and always would, even if there might be an ocean between them . . .

If only she could go to see Sawyer.

But to do so meant seeing Remington too, and that, she wasn't ready to do.

Anna Vanderhoff sat at the opposite end of the table from her husband, playing her part as hostess with the ease born of years of practice. The guests to her right and to her left never felt neglected. She engaged them in conversation, encouraging them to talk about themselves, laughing when appropriate, all the while keeping an eye on the servants as they brought each course, watching to see that wineglasses were filled and no one was in want of anything.

But it was her daughter who captured her thoughts.

Anna felt as though her heart were breaking in two as she remembered the way her beloved child had looked upon her return to Rosegate. She'd seen the utter desolation in Olivia's eyes of green. Something had happened to her in Idaho, something that had sent her back to New York without a fight, something beyond being found by Northrop's detectives.

If only Olivia would talk about it, tell Anna what had happened. But her daughter had retreated within herself, and nothing Anna said or did had penetrated the barrier.

Again she looked down the length of the long table, the white tablecloth covered with fine china and silver, crystal goblets, and candelabra with long, tapered candles. She looked at her husband. *What have you done, Northrop? What have you done to Olivia?*

"It appears the viscount is quite taken with your daughter, Mrs. Vanderhoff," the guest at her right commented.

Anna's gaze returned to Olivia, this time taking in Spencer Lambert too. "Yes, it does."

If Northrop had his way — and when did he not? — their daughter would be a countess. Olivia Lambert, Countess of Northcliffe. But would she be happy? Olivia's happiness mattered more to Anna than titles or castles in England.

If only you would tell me what happened, dearest.

Sawyer heard the door to his bedroom open and sat up as Remington stepped into the room.

"Sawyer?"

"Yeah."

"Sorry to wake you."

"I wasn't asleep."

Remington sat on the edge of the bed. "I've got an idea."

"To get Libby to talk to you?"

"Yes. But I'll need your help."

Sawyer nodded his consent without even hearing the plan. After all, that's why they'd come to this city. So Remington could tell Libby he was sorry and then they could all go back to the Blue Springs.

When Sawyer first learned Libby was gone, he'd felt mighty bad. He was even a little angry at her 'cause she'd promised him she was gonna always be there for him, and then she'd left without even saying good-bye. But Remington had helped Sawyer see it wasn't Libby's fault. "I'm to blame, Sawyer," he'd said before telling him the whole story.

Not a day had gone by since then that Sawyer didn't ask God to show him and Remington what to do to get Libby back. Remington prayed too, and Sawyer didn't doubt the Lord heard their requests. If Remington had a plan, then Sawyer reckoned the Lord was behind it.

"So what do you need me to do, Rem? I'm ready, whatever it is."

Twenty-Seven

"WHAT ABOUT THE EMERALD GOWN, Miss Olivia? It's so pretty with your hair."

Olivia glanced over her shoulder as her maid drew the velvet dress from the wardrobe. "It doesn't matter, Sophie. Choose whatever you like."

Sophie clucked her tongue. "Doesn't matter, she says. And you going out in the viscount's carriage for one and all to see. There's not an unmarried girl in all Manhattan who doesn't wish she was in your shoes, and you saying it doesn't matter what you wear. Why, you've got more new gowns than you could wear in a month. There must be something that catches your fancy."

Without reply, Olivia turned again and stared at the changing leaves in the trees beyond the window. If she closed her eyes, she could see aspens cloaked in gold. But she didn't close her eyes because she didn't want to see aspens.

"You'd better hurry, Miss Olivia. His Lordship will be here soon, and you know what your father will be like if you keep the viscount waiting."

"Yes, Sophie. I know."

"And come back from that window. Have you forgotten you're wearing only your corset and petticoats?"

Olivia was about to do as the maid had bid when a small figure caught her attention. A boy with dark brown hair, his hands shoved in his pockets. He stood across the street from the Vanderhoff mansion, staring at the house. She leaned forward, nearly touching her forehead to the glass.

"Sawyer," she whispered.

As if he'd heard her, he raised his arm and waved. She waved back, then placed her hand on the window, wishing . . .

She whirled around. "Hurry, Sophie. Help me into my gown."

The maid looked surprised by Olivia's change of mood, but she did as she was told, lifting up the gown and slipping it over her mistress's head, then quickly fastening it up the back.

Olivia reached for the matching hat and smashed it onto her head, tucking back loose strands of hair, then tying a hasty bow beneath her right ear.

"Your hair, miss. We haven't — "

"It doesn't matter, Sophie. My hat will hide it."

"But, Miss Olivia — "

She grabbed the green reticule Sophie had set out, not bothering to see if a handkerchief had been placed inside. Then she slipped her feet into her new walking shoes and rushed toward the door.

She moved as quickly as possible along the hall and down the stairs, praying her father wasn't waiting for her in the front parlor. Givens, the butler, was passing through the entry hall as Olivia reached the bottom of the stairs. With a finger to her lips, she begged him for silence, then hurried toward the front door, not stopping until she was outside.

Her eyes sought the familiar figure across the street. But all she saw was Spencer Lambert's spider phaeton coming down Seventy-second Street toward Rosegate. Olivia scarcely spared the viscount a glance as she searched up and then down the street, but Sawyer was nowhere to be seen.

Her heart sank. She was too late. She'd missed him. It took her too long to dress. He must think she didn't want to see him. Would another opportunity present itself? She'd been fortunate to get out the door this time without being stopped by her father.

As Spencer's phaeton drew to a halt, the groom jumped down from the skeleton rumble and hurried to hold the reins while the viscount descended from the driver's seat.

"Miss Vanderhoff, what a surprise to find you waiting for me outside." He gave her a smile. "I never cease to be amazed by the freedom you American girls enjoy. You will need to curb those tendencies when you come to England."

You are a pompous man, Lord Lambert. Nothing is settled between us.

It was the first spark of life she'd felt in over two months, but she hid her irritation behind a look of wide-eyed innocence. "To be honest, sir, I'd forgotten you were calling. Did we have an engagement?"

Her remark removed the self-satisfied smirk from his mouth. "Indeed we did. We were to go for a drive in Central Park. I hope you have not made other plans."

Sudden inspiration made her swallow the comment that would have sent him away. Instead she offered what she hoped was a conciliatory smile. "Not at all, Lord Lambert. I was taking a bit of air. I'd much rather go for a drive in your carriage . . . with you." She took hold of his arm. "Come into the house and say hello to Father while I get my muff. Then we can be on our way."

Olivia endured the drive through Central Park with cloaked impatience. It wasn't until the carriage was headed back to Rosegate that she touched the viscount's arm with her gloved fingers. "Lord Lambert, would you do me a tremendous favor?"

"Of course, Miss Vanderhoff. If it's within my power."

"Might we stop by a friend's house? Just for a moment. I promise not to tarry long."

"Naturally. I'll be glad to oblige. And you needn't hurry. Nothing could please me more than to prolong our time together." He covered her hand with his own. "Just point the way. I'm not well acquainted with the streets of your fair city."

Remington frowned when he saw Libby sitting beside the English dandy, her cheeks and nose pink from the crisp fall air. He hadn't expected her to call with Lord Lambert — the man the gossips predicted was to become her husband — in tow.

Not if I have anything to say about it. He turned from the window. "Sawyer, Libby's here."

The boy descended the stairs, sounding like a stampeding herd of wild horses. When he reached the parlor window and looked out, he frowned. "Who's that man with her?" Sawyer sounded as displeased about the viscount as Remington felt.

"An English lord looking for a wife." The plain fact tasted sour on his tongue.

"He's gonna marry Libby?"

Remington watched the viscount assist her from the carriage. "No." He looked at Sawyer. "You know what to do?"

The boy nodded.

"All right." He squeezed Sawyer's shoulder. "Good luck." Remington headed toward the door at the back of his home, calling as he went, "Mrs. Blake, I'll be out for the afternoon."

Perhaps I shouldn't have come, Olivia thought before the door opened.

"Yes?" The plump woman who greeted her had rosy red cheeks and wore a crisp white apron.

"Is this" — the question caught in her throat for a moment, and she felt a familiar sting in her heart — "the Walker residence?"

"Yes, it is, but Mr. Walker isn't in. I'm Mrs. Blake, the housekeeper. May I leave a message for him?"

Relief gave Olivia courage. "I've come to see Sawyer Deevers. Is he at home?"

The door opened wider. "He is, miss. May I tell him who's calling?"

What was the answer to that question? She wasn't certain anymore. Glancing over her shoulder at Spencer who waited in the carriage, she said, "I'm Miss Vanderhoff. Tell Sawyer I'm a friend of Libby Blue's."

"Please, come in, Miss Vanderhoff." Mrs. Blake showed Olivia into the parlor. "I'll tell Master Sawyer you're here." Then she left the room.

I shouldn't have come. It will hurt more after I see him.

She let her gaze wander over the furniture. This was Remington's home. This was where he lived, where he slept, where he ate. She could almost feel his presence.

I shouldn't have come.

"Libby!"

She whirled around and stared at the boy in the doorway. It seemed Sawyer had shot up several inches since she saw him last. With his trimmed hair and new clothes, he looked much older than the boy she'd left behind. He looked ... wonderful.

Hot tears filled her throat, and she swallowed hard. She hadn't cried. Not in all these weeks. Not even once.

"Hello, Sawyer," she said, barely above a whisper. "Was that you I saw outside my window this morning?"

He nodded. "I wanted to see you."

"I wanted to see you too."

He shot across the room and threw himself into her arms, hugging her tightly. "I've missed you, Libby."

She couldn't stop the tears from falling. "I've missed you too."

Sawyer pulled back and looked into her eyes. Then he reached up and brushed the tears from her cheeks with his thumb. "You oughta come back to the Blue Springs. You ain't happy here."

"Aren't happy."

"Aren't happy. And you *aren't* happy ... are you?" But it wasn't really a question.

Olivia forced a tiny smile. "You don't understand, Sawyer. It's so very complicated."

"Remington told me everything. He's sorry. He wants you to come home with us."

She straightened, turned away. *Home.* She mouthed the word. Her chest hurt.

"I want you t'come home too."

She walked to the window and gazed at the carriage waiting for her at the curb. She looked at Spencer Lambert, the man her father wanted her to marry. And so she would marry him, because she wasn't strong enough to fight her father any longer.

Remington's betrayal hurt deeply. She couldn't bear to be hurt again. "I can't go back to the Blue Springs, Sawyer."

"You're wrong, Libby," a deep, familiar voice said from behind her. "You could go. Your father couldn't stop you."

She closed her eyes. *I won't feel. I won't think. I won't let him touch me or hurt me.* She didn't have to turn around to know Remington had moved closer. She felt him entering the room.

"I'm glad you came, Libby."

She turned, holding herself stiff and straight.

Remington stood in Sawyer's place. "I need to explain, Libby. You owe me a chance to explain."

"I don't *owe* you anything, Mr. Walker."

"I didn't tell your father I'd found you. I sent him a telegram saying he should give up the search, that I couldn't find you. I didn't want his money. Not after I fell in love with you. My plan was to sell this house and my agency so I could pay your father back everything. I swear it's true."

"You, Mr. Walker, are an accomplished liar."

"I never lied about loving you."

"You never said you loved me until last week. I only thought you had."

"I wanted to make things right first."

"And how were you going to do that?" Not waiting for an answer, she stepped around him and walked toward the entry.

"I'm not giving up," Remington called after her. "We have something between us that is too special to lose."

She stopped and turned. "*We* have nothing between us."

"Ask your father to show you my telegram."

He'd lied to her about who he was, about why he'd come to the Blue Springs. He'd lied about his home in Virginia. Why did he persist in heaping more lies on top of those that had gone before? Why couldn't he let her be?

The anger drained from her, leaving her tired, so tired she wondered if she could make it to the phaeton. Her shoulders drooped, and her reticule felt like a heavy weight, pulling on her arm.

"If you really loved me," she said softly, "you would leave me in peace." She turned again. "Tell Sawyer I'm sorry."

Northrop was in a fury when he descended from his carriage that evening and strode up the front steps at Rosegate. Flinging the door open, he bellowed, "Olivia!"

Anna appeared in the doorway of the parlor, looking alarmed. "Northrop, what is it?"

"Where's that daughter of mine?"

"I believe she's in her room. But what in heaven's name is — "

"Olivia!" He stared up the dark-paneled staircase. "Get down here." Turning to his wife, he said, "Send her to my study. I'll wait for her there."

"But, Northrop — "

He ignored her, striding down the hallway.

He would not allow it. He would not allow Olivia to defy him again. If he had to lock her in the house, in her room, then so be it. He would make a prisoner of her if he must.

Olivia arrived just as he settled onto the chair behind his desk. "You wanted to see me, Father?"

"Come in and sit down."

She did as she was told.

Northrop leaned forward in his chair. "Is it true?"

"Is what true, Father?"

"Has that detective returned to New York? Have you seen Walker?"

There wasn't so much as a flicker of emotion on her face. "Yes."

Northrop slammed his hands on his desk and rose from his chair. "I won't have it! You'll not jeopardize your marriage prospects by consorting with that man. Do you want the whole world to know how I found you? You're going to stay away from him. Do you hear me?"

"You needn't shout, Father." She stood, looking cool, regal, remote. "I have no interest in *consorting* with Mr. Walker." Without waiting for his dismissal, she turned and walked toward the door. Before reaching it, she paused and glanced behind her. "Has Lord Lambert asked for your permission to marry me?"

Her question surprised him. "Not yet, but I expect he will soon."

"I see. Will it be necessary for us to have a long engagement?"

"I suppose not."

"Good." She disappeared into the hallway.

Frowning, Northrop stared after her. The interview had not turned out as he expected. When he heard today that Remington Walker was back in the city and had been seen talking to Olivia at the Harrisons' soiree, he suspected trouble was afoot.

He sank onto his chair, steepling his hands in front of his face.

He wasn't a fool. He'd known the moment he saw Olivia at that miserable ranch that his daughter wasn't the naive, pliable girl who'd run away from Manhattan. She did seem earnest now in her proclaimed disinterest, but Northrop wasn't convinced it would last. Not when the man moved in the same social circle as the Vanderhoffs.

He could possibly discredit Walker, but it would be risky. He didn't want to ruin Olivia's reputation at the same time, not when others might learn it was Walker who found her. The fabricated story of her sick friend could be exposed for the fiction it was. The truth would ruin everything.

He tapped his forefingers together, staring into space.

It seemed Olivia's plan was best: get her married to the viscount and packed off to London as soon as possible. Northrop stood to gain plenty from an alliance with the

Lambert family and the influence it would bring the Vanderhoffs in England and throughout the British Empire. This arrangement, in fact, would be far more valuable than the railroad he'd lost seven years ago. After the wedding, Remington Walker could be dealt with in an appropriate manner.

Yes, he would have to speed along Spencer Lambert's courtship of Olivia. The quicker the two of them married, the better.

Twenty-Eight

THE LAST OF THE SEASON'S roses bloomed in the Rosegate gardens even as sharp autumn winds rattled drying leaves loose from tree branches and sent them rolling across the ground. But Anna noticed neither the wind nor the fading blossoms as she strolled among the rosebushes a week after Northrop's outburst.

Anna's concern for her daughter mounted with each passing day. Two days ago the future earl made his coveted proposal, and Olivia accepted without hesitation or joy. The *New York Times* announced the match in yesterday's edition. Today a steady stream of well-wishers arrived at Rosegate, many of them expressing friendly envy. Olivia seemed content, but trouble pricked Anna's heart. Appearances could be deceiving.

Olivia wasn't in love with Spencer Lambert, nor did the viscount love Olivia. And Anna so wanted her daughter to be in love. Happily in love. She wanted Olivia to have so much more than an arranged marriage founded on the empty values of wealth, property, and position.

She stopped and stared toward the house. Rosegate had been one of the first large mansions built in Manhattan at a time when most Knickerbockers were content to reside in their modest, comfortably uniform brownstones.

But Northrop had never known contentment. He wanted great wealth and power, beyond what his father possessed. And he'd achieved it too, thanks more than a little to the hardship that befell others during the Civil War.

Anna first met the dashing Mr. Vanderhoff during those war years. They were introduced at a ball to benefit the wounded soldiers of the Union army. Within days of Northrop's first call at her home, she thought herself in love with him. During their few chaperoned meetings together, she fell completely under his spell.

"I was so young," she whispered. "So naive."

She didn't see beyond Northrop's handsome veneer. Not once did she inquire about his likes or dislikes. Not once did she question if the two of them were well suited. Worse still, she never broached the subject of faith, even though belief in God was important to her.

Anna sank onto a concrete bench and folded her hands. "'And we know that all things work together for good to them that love God, to them who are the called according to his purpose.'"

She released a sigh. Perhaps the difficulties in her life, in her marriage, had strengthened her faith, deepened her love of God, ensured her dependence upon Him. And yet Anna felt she had compromised her faith too often, using some misunderstood notion of submission as an excuse to do nothing when she should have acted. Had she set a godly example for her daughter? Did Olivia know what was important in a marriage, or did she see it only as a duty, as an obligation, even something to be feared?

Another verse from the Bible entered her thoughts, one that seemed brand new to her when she read it that morning:

And unto the married I command, yet not I, but the Lord, Let not the wife depart from her husband: But and if she depart, let her remain unmarried, or be reconciled to her husband.

God hated divorce — as did society. And the apostle Peter had also written that a wife's submissive behavior might win an unbelieving husband to Christ. For years, those two Scriptures were first and foremost in her thoughts, even when she learned of Northrop's affairs, even when she learned he had illegitimate children, even when he struck her.

But and if she depart, let her remain unmarried. Anna straightened on the bench. "I would not want to marry again."

Father, even if Your Word gives me leave to separate because of Northrop's adultery, where would I go? I have no one. I have nothing. I'm unable even to protect my daughter.

She pulled her cloak more tightly about her, feeling the wind cut through the wool cloth, chilling her to the bone. She remembered the yellow gown, still wrapped in tissue and hidden in a box beneath her bed. That dress symbolized all that was wrong with her marriage and with her life. Somehow she had to protect Olivia from the same future, from the same failure.

As she did so often of late, Olivia stood at her third-story bedroom window. A delivery wagon moved along Seventy-second Street, headed toward Madison Avenue.

Madison Avenue. Where Remington lived.

"I never lied about loving you . . ."

But he had. He had lied.

"I'm not giving up. We have something between us that is too special to lose..."

But there wasn't anything between them. Not anymore. She would marry Spencer Lambert. She would leave America and live in England, where everything was different and she could forget.

Let him kiss me with the kisses of his mouth: for thy love is better than wine. The words from the Song of Solomon tormented her.

Tears welled in her eyes. "Remington." She hated him for making her remember all that she had felt for him. She hated him for overpowering her resolve not to cry. She preferred the numbness, the safety of a stone-cold heart, the absence of feeling.

"Ask your father to show you my telegram..."

She covered her ears with her hands and squeezed her eyes closed. "Leave me alone. Please, leave me alone."

But he was there, in her head, in her heart. *"I never lied about loving you..."*

She heard the knock on her door but ignored it. She wanted no more congratulations, no more comments about her good fortune.

"Olivia?" The door opened. "Dearest?"

She lowered her hands from her ears and turned to face her mother.

"May I come in?"

"Of course."

Her mother closed the door behind her, then crossed the room, reaching out to take Olivia's hand. "Sit with me for a moment, will you? We must talk."

"Oh, Mama . . ."

"Please, dear."

Reluctantly she allowed her mother to draw her to the sofa near one of the two fireplaces in her bedchamber. In unison, they sat down.

Her mother's light blue eyes searched Olivia's face for a long while before she spoke. "I want you to tell me what happened while you were gone from New York."

"It isn't important."

"Yes, it is. I think it's very important."

Olivia glanced toward the window.

Her mother's grip tightened on her hand. "Olivia, don't do this to yourself. Don't hide from the truth." Her voice grew soft. "Don't be like me."

Olivia looked at her mother again.

Anna leaned forward. "Listen to me. I know what it means to withdraw inside yourself. I've hidden from the truth for so many years, it's become second nature to me. But that's no way to live."

She kissed her mother's cheek but remained silent.

"Who is he?" Anna asked. "The man you love."

Olivia shook her head, as if to deny such a man existed.

"Tell me about him, dear."

Tears trickled down Olivia's cheeks.

"It might help to talk about him," her mother encouraged.

"It won't help. Nothing will help."

Anna gathered her into her arms, pressing Olivia's head against her chest. "Oh, my darling daughter, tell me what has happened. Tell me what has hurt you so deeply."

The words began to pour out of her then, just as the tears streamed down her cheeks. She told her mother about Amanda

Blue and the Blue Springs Ranch, about Dan and Sawyer Deevers, about Alistair McGregor and Ronald Aberdeen, about old Lightning and Misty and her pups, about Pete and Lynette Fisher, even about Timothy Bevins.

Then, in a halting voice, she told her mother about Remington, about falling in love with him, about his betrayal.

For a long time after Olivia fell silent, after her tears were dry, her mother held her, rocking her gently. Then she said, "Olivia, you must tell the viscount you cannot marry him. You must break it off before it's too late."

"It's already too late. I'm going to marry and go to England."

Her mother took her by the shoulders and held her at arm's length. "Mr. Walker didn't lie to you about the telegram. I saw it. He told your father to give up looking for you. He told Northrop you couldn't be found."

A breathless *no* escaped Olivia's parted lips.

"It's true. I promise you, it's true."

From his office in the Vanderhoff Shipping warehouse on the East River, Northrop could see Governors Island, the Statue of Liberty, and Ellis Island. Churning its way through the choppy, whitecapped river, the Fulton ferry headed toward its slip on South Street. Tall sails waved over ships docked at piers lining the riverbank, and smoke belched from chimneys above the low, steep-roofed loft buildings of lower Manhattan.

Northrop rarely visited the warehouse these days, though when he was a lad, he had often joined his grandfather here.

Even then he'd dreamed of Vanderhoff warehouses in ports around the world, and he'd seen those dreams come true through the years. Now Olivia's marriage to Lord Lambert would expand his empire even farther.

He laughed. To think he'd been willing to settle for a railroad from Gregory James. A railroad was something he could buy. In fact, he now owned all the American railroads he needed.

It seemed Olivia had done him a favor by bolting all those years ago. It hadn't occurred to him back then to look beyond New York for a son-in-law, not until he'd witnessed for himself the number of American heiresses marrying titled Englishmen. Now his daughter would be a countess and the mother of earls, and Northrop would profit.

He frowned as his thoughts turned to Remington Walker. Why had the detective sought out Olivia at the Harrisons' soiree? Northrop didn't doubt that Olivia once fancied herself in love with the man. Had Walker hoped to rekindle the alliance upon his return to New York? Had he actually hoped to marry Olivia and get himself a piece of Vanderhoff Shipping?

Well, it didn't matter. Olivia was willingly engaged and would soon be wed. Unless Walker was a fool, he would keep silent about the part he played in Olivia Vanderhoff's return to Manhattan. And if he was a fool, Northrop would find a way to silence him.

Turning away from the grimy window, he reached for his hat and walking stick, then headed for the door. He considered going to see Ellen but discarded the idea. There was little pleasure to be found with her these days. Even after all these weeks, his mistress had yet to forgive him for sending his sons away to school. Her anger was evident in her eyes, in her words, even in her bed.

His wife was no more pleasant. Something about Anna had changed over the summer months, although he wasn't quite sure what.

He clenched his jaw as he settled against the plush seat of his carriage. Why were the women in his life so bent on making him miserable?

Olivia stared at her mother, unable to believe what she'd heard. Not daring to believe it.

Anna took hold of Olivia's hands and squeezed them. "Go talk to Mr. Walker. He must love you. He tried to protect you."

She shook her head.

"You can't marry Lord Lambert, not if you love another man."

Her throat burned, and she found it difficult to speak. "Father has forbidden me to see Remington."

"God will help you find a way if you ask Him." Her mother rose from the sofa, allowing Olivia's hands to slip from her fingers. "At least think about what I've said." She walked toward the door, accompanied by a whisper of rustling petticoats.

After the door closed, Olivia turned her gaze upon the fire blazing on the hearth, a small voice of hope whispering in her ear, *Remington didn't tell Father where I was. Remington didn't lie about that.*

Her mother was right. She had to talk to Remington. She had to listen to his explanation. She had to know the truth.

She closed her eyes. For the first time in months, she allowed memories of Remington, of Sawyer, and of the Blue Springs Ranch to come. She allowed the memories to flood over her, indulging every image.

If it was true . . . if Remington hadn't betrayed her . . . if he truly did love her . . .

She hugged herself, wanting to believe, for the first time in many weeks, allowing herself to hope.

Twenty-Nine

REMINGTON SET THE LATEST EDITION of the *New York Times* on the table and looked about the large room of his private club. Businessmen and the idle rich sat in comfortable chairs, most of them reading their newspapers and smoking their pipes or cigars. He wondered how many of them were well-enough connected to receive an invitation to Libby's wedding.

The thought set his teeth on edge.

During the past week, he had tried everything short of storming the doors of Rosegate in order to see her, but their paths had not crossed again. Now that her engagement to Lord Lambert had been formally announced, his hope waned.

"If you really loved me, you would leave me in peace . . ."

His fist tightened as he heard her words again in his head, remembered the weariness in the way she carried herself. He'd done that to her. He'd put the sadness in her beautiful eyes.

"Remington Walker. What luck!"

He glanced up to find Charlton Bernard standing before him.

"I wonder if you might do me a favor." Charlton sat on a nearby chair. "My sister — you remember Lillian — is having a supper tonight for a few friends, and she has come up short one gentleman. She made me swear on my life that I wouldn't return from the club without someone to round out her guest list. Do say you'll come."

Remington was about to decline, but Charlton didn't give him a chance.

"This is Lillian's first night to shine since her wedding last summer. She and her husband have moved into their new home, and Lillian has run the servants into the ground in preparation for her debut as a hostess. You may have heard that Lord Lambert and his fiancée will be there. Quite an accomplishment for my baby sister. Of course, Mother was none too pleased that Miss Vanderhoff chose to marry that viscount instead of her darling son" — Charlton grinned — "but the old girl's putting up a good front for Lillian's sake." His smile disappeared. "Listen, I know this is terribly poor form to invite you like this, but it would be a tremendous help."

Remington only half heard what the man said. He'd stopped listening the moment he learned Libby would be there. "I'd be glad to come."

"Splendid! Here's Lillian's address." He gave Remington a card. "Dinner will be at eight. See you then." Charlton rose and walked away.

Remington stared at the card in his hand and said a quick thanks to God.

⟨ornament⟩

As usual, Olivia let her maid select what she would wear for the evening, but now the reason for her indifference had changed. How could she care about clothes when all that mattered was Remington: to see him, to talk to him, to listen at last to the truth? If only she could find a way to slip out from under her father's watchful eye.

As if he knew she'd had a change of heart, Northrop hadn't left Rosegate for the past twenty-four hours. It seemed he was always nearby, watching and listening. Her only sanctuary was her own room.

"You'll look lovely in this gown, Miss Olivia," Sophie said as she carried it across the room. "Green really is the best color for you, and this a Worth. It's no wonder every lady wants her gowns ordered from Paris. Even Mrs. Davenport cannot equal this fine work."

Olivia didn't spare the dress a glance. She simply raised her arms and allowed the maid to lift it over her head and drop it down. The fabric, cool and smooth, whispered over her corset and linen chemise, her cotton drawers, and her dark green stockings. She turned and faced the cheval glass, which reflected her lack of interest as Sophie fastened the closing up her back.

A sash of black watered ribbon cinched the graceful gown of nile green china crepe, and a garniture of pink blossoms adorned her waist. Shirred gauze covered the low, square corsage, and an epaulet of pink flowers rode her left shoulder. The look was new, flattering, and fashionable.

How she missed her trousers and boots! And she hated the pinch of the corset around her rib cage. She longed to draw a deep breath without feeling hindered.

"Your shoes, Miss Olivia." Sophie scooted the green evening slippers closer to her feet.

Olivia put on the shoes, then moved to the stool in front of her vanity table and sat down so Sophie could dress her hair.

Twisting her engagement ring on her finger, she remained silent. How was she to see Remington as long as her father watched her like a hawk? She couldn't ask Spencer to take her to Remington's house again, and she wasn't sure whom she could trust among the servants. Their employer was ruthless. Could she ask any of them to risk their position by taking a note to Remington? Would she trust the wrong person and find she'd been reported to her father?

"Miss Olivia, I wonder if I might ask something of you."

She met Sophie's gaze in the mirror. "What is it?"

"When you go to England after the wedding, I was wondering if you might take me along as your maid? You see, my grandmother still lives there. I haven't seen her since I was a little girl. Now that my parents have both passed on, I'd like very much to see her again. She's all the family I've got left in the world."

Maybe she could trust Sophie with a message to Remington, in exchange for helping her get to England. Maybe this was the opportunity she'd been hoping for.

"I'll do what I can, Sophie. I promise." *But with any luck, you'll go to England without me.*

Upon Alfred and Lillian Cameron's return from their European honeymoon, they set up housekeeping in a modest four-story brownstone on Lexington Avenue, a few blocks from the Episcopal Church of the Epiphany. Eighteen and pretty, Lillian welcomed Remington Walker to the Cameron house with a nervous smile and the look of a new bride who feared she might fail as a hostess.

"Thank you for joining us, Mr. Walker. I appreciate your graciousness."

"It's my pleasure, Mrs. Cameron."

Ten minutes later, when Libby appeared in the doorway, her hand on Spencer Lambert's arm, Remington chanced to find himself alone, which gave him the opportunity to watch her with an unfettered gaze. The gown she wore was exquisite, as was the emerald necklace gracing her throat. Her complexion was milk white, without even a hint of freckles on her nose and cheeks.

I miss your freckles, Libby. And I hate the sadness in your eyes. Am I the only one who sees it?

As if she'd heard him, she looked up. Their gazes met and, for a breathless moment, held. Remington expected her to turn away. He did not expect a tentative smile.

But there it was, curving her mouth at the corners.

She whispered something to the viscount, then drew him across the room toward Remington. "Mr. Walker, it's a pleasure to see you again."

Was this some sort of joke?

"May I introduce Spencer Lambert, Viscount Chelsea."

Was this how she intended to punish him for his perfidy, by flaunting her fiancé in front of him?

She glanced at the man beside her. "Spencer, this is Remington Walker. His father, I've heard, raised some of the finest horses in the South before the war. Mr. Walker has continued the tradition since his move to Manhattan."

Remington scarcely looked at the viscount as the two men shook hands.

"It's always a pleasure to meet one of Olivia's friends," Spencer said. "Perhaps you'll show me your livestock one day."

"Yes. To be sure." Who cared about horses at a time like this? What was it he saw in Libby's expression?

She swept her gaze over the room. "Oh, look, Spencer. There's Penelope and Alexander." She faced Remington again. "Please excuse us, Mr. Walker, but we must say hello to the Harrisons."

"Of course."

The couple started away, but Libby stopped and turned back, whispering, "I must talk to you. Alone."

The evening was long and torturous as Remington awaited the opportunity for that talk. It came after supper when the gentlemen went off to smoke and the ladies retired to the parlor. With only a glance exchanged between them, Remington and Olivia slipped away from the others and up the stairs. They met in a small sitting room on the second floor. A gas lamp, turned low, provided a source of light as they faced each other.

Olivia, her stomach aflutter with nerves, was suddenly uncertain how to begin. Finally she asked, "How is Sawyer?"

"He's fine. He misses you." His eyes studied her with increasing intensity.

"Remington, I . . ." She licked her dry lips with her tongue. "Remington, I . . . I want you to tell me again what happened. Between you and my father. I . . . I want to know the truth, and this time I promise to listen. I want to know everything. I *need* to know."

He reached for her hand, but she took a step backward, out of reach, as if his touch might cause her fragile hope to crumble, to shatter into a thousand pieces.

When he spoke, his tone was gentle. "All right, Libby." He motioned toward two chairs. "Come and sit down. It's a long story."

She led the way, settling onto the edge of a carved rosewood chair while her heart thumped a deafening beat.

Remington raked the fingers of one hand through his hair, a small frown drawing his brows together. "It's hard to know where to begin."

Tell me you love me. Begin there. But that would be the wrong place to start. She needed the truth even more than words of love.

"Did you know our fathers were business acquaintances years ago? Friends even. At least my father thought they were friends." He didn't wait for a reply. "That was before the war."

She listened as he recounted the story of Northrop and Jefferson, about the years before and after the Civil War, about Jefferson's despair and suicide. She wasn't shocked by the part her father had played in the ruination of Jefferson Walker and the JW Railroad.

"When your father called me to Rosegate and asked me to find you, I thought at first it was because he knew who I was. I thought it might be his way of making some sort of amends. But I believe he's forgotten my father. When I demanded the bonus if I found you before the end of a year, I never expected him to agree, but once he did, I knew this was my chance to exact revenge. I couldn't destroy him as he destroyed my father, but I could hurt him. I could take his money. In time, I could buy enough stock in his company to endanger his control."

An invisible band tightened around her chest, making each breath she drew painful.

Remington stared into a dark corner of the room. "When I awakened at the Blue Springs and saw you for the first time, I knew even then that it would be hard to send you back to your father. I could see you were content there. But I'd promised the memory of my father that I would seek retribution. I wanted to get well and send that telegram and return to New York. I wanted to get out of Idaho as quickly as possible." He brought his eyes back to meet hers. "But I fell in love with you, Libby, and money didn't matter anymore. Revenge didn't matter. It's like God reached down and cut that need right out of my heart. Nothing mattered except being with you. When I went to Weiser with Pete Fisher, I sent your father a telegram saying I'd failed, that you couldn't be found. I told him to give up his search."

"How did he find me, then? Why did he try to pay you that money?"

"He had me followed. He hired another detective to find me when I didn't send my usual report." His eyes narrowed, sparking with anger. "And he gave me that check to make sure you wouldn't stay with me. He's a shrewd man, your father."

It sounded plausible. It could be true. "Why wouldn't you marry me right away?" she whispered, then swallowed the sudden tears that burned the back of her throat. "Why did you put it off?"

"I didn't want your father to come between us. I didn't want to owe him anything, not even the fee he paid me before I left Manhattan. That's why I was going to sell everything, including my house. To pay him back. I wanted things to be right before we married."

"But you didn't tell me the truth. You didn't tell me who you really were. You let me believe you lived at Sunnyvale. You let me believe so many things that weren't true."

He leaned forward. "No, I didn't tell you the truth, and I was wrong. I shouldn't have kept silent. I should have explained everything. But there were so many lies between us, and I was afraid you would hate me when you learned the truth, so I put it off."

"You were afraid?"

"Afraid I'd lose you." He took hold of her hand, and this time she didn't pull away.

She closed her eyes. "I'm afraid too."

His fingers tightened. "I love you, Libby. I want to marry you. I want to take you back to the Blue Springs. We were happy there. We could be happy again."

She looked at him. He'd lied to her about so much, but then, she was guilty of lying too. Wasn't she as much at fault as he? Could they put everything behind them? Could she learn to trust him again?

God, what should I do?

She slipped her hand free of his and rose from the chair. "I'd better return before I'm missed. Father watches my every move."

"Don't let him force you into a marriage you don't want, Libby. Even if you can't love me, don't let him do that to you."

I do love you, her heart confessed. But she couldn't tell him so. Her father controlled her fate. Better not tell Remington she loved him if they would never be together.

Olivia shook her head slowly, then turned and left the room.

Rosegate was quiet, the windows darkened, by the time the Lambert carriage brought Olivia home. Spencer escorted her into the entry, where he helped her out of her cloak.

"Is something troubling you, Olivia?" He took hold of her elbows and turned her to face him. "You've been inordinately quiet this evening."

She couldn't meet his gaze. "No, Spencer. I'm simply tired."

"Well, then, I shall let you retire." He gave her a perfunctory kiss on the cheek. "Sleep well, my dear."

"Thank you. Good night."

As soon as the door closed, Olivia picked up the lamp that stood on a table in the entry and started up the stairs. But she paused before she'd gone far.

"I sent your father a telegram saying I'd failed, that you couldn't be found ..."

She looked down the hallway toward her father's study.

"Olivia, Mr. Walker didn't lie to you about the telegram. I saw it ..."

She descended the stairs.

The study was her father's sanctuary, his most private domain. He allowed neither Olivia nor her mother to enter the room unless summoned there. With an unsteady hand, Olivia turned the knob and pushed open the door.

A flood of bad memories washed over her as she stared into the dark room. She saw herself as she'd once been, a lonely child, seeking her father's approval and affection. She saw the wounded girl who wondered why her father couldn't love her.

It's not my fault.

Her pulse quickened.

It's not my fault he can't love me.

She stepped into the room, moving toward the massive desk.

Father doesn't love anyone. He loves only money and power. It's not my fault.

A sigh whispered through her lips, and with the corresponding intake of air, she felt a sudden release. Fear of the future — and of her father — seemed to flee from her. No matter what she found tonight, she didn't have to be afraid anymore.

She sat in the large chair behind the desk, placed the lamp on the desktop, and pulled open the top drawer. She drew in another deep breath, then began her search.

It was nearly four in the morning before she found the two telegrams, both of them folded and wrinkled.

She read the first through a blur of tears:

```
no sign of olivia in idaho stop trail is
cold stop suggest you forego further
search stop walker
```

She skimmed the second telegram, her heart racing with joy as she read the only words that mattered:

```
found walker and olivia stop will await
you in weiser idaho stop send instruc-
tions care of weiser hotel stop o'reilly
```

Remington didn't betray me to my father. She covered her face with shaking hands. *He didn't lie about loving me.*

Tomorrow morning she would go to him. Tomorrow she would tell Remington she loved him.

Tomorrow.

Thirty

OLIVIA AWOKE WITH A START. Anemic morning light peeked around the window curtains, announcing the coming of dawn.

Remington!

Tossing aside the blankets, she slid her legs over to the side of the high poster bed. Her hair tumbled into her face, and she pushed it back with an impatient hand. She didn't ring for Sophie, intending to dress herself. There had to be something in her wardrobe she could manage without the help of her maid.

She hurried across the room and stirred up the fire on the hearth, adding more fuel. Then she performed hasty morning ablutions in the connecting bathing chamber. From her vast wardrobe, she chose a dark blue gown with buttons up the front of the bodice.

Hurry. Hurry. Hurry.

Her bodice fastened, she turned to the mirror and picked up her hairbrush, knowing she would never be able to dress her hair as Sophie would.

Remington likes it braided.

She smiled. Remington liked her hair in a braid, and so did she. With brisk strokes of the brush, she swept the tangles from her hair, then wove it into one thick plait, tying the end with a ribbon. How natural and wonderful it felt. And she no longer saw Olivia Vanderhoff staring back at her from the mirror. She saw Libby, and her heart sang with joy because Remington loved Libby Blue.

Still wearing his evening attire, Remington watched from the window of his bedchamber as dawn spilled shades of pink and lavender across the clouds on the horizon. He watched it and wondered when he might hear from Libby again.

"Father watches my every move."

He turned away from the window, raking the fingers of both hands through his hair. He shouldn't have let her leave the Camerons' home last night. He should have dragged her, if need be, back to his place. He should have held her and kissed her until she couldn't think of anything but him.

When would he see her again? How could he discover her thoughts if they couldn't meet?

Church! This was Sunday. She would be at church.

He glanced at the clock on the mantel. The Vanderhoff women attended the Presbyterian church no more than a dozen blocks from his brownstone. He'd learned that bit of information when he first took Northrop's case. It was equally well known that Northrop never darkened a church door, having no use for religion. If Remington hurried, he could arrive before the service began.

Libby placed the dark blue bonnet on her head, her thoughts far away. She imagined Remington's face as she told him she was sorry for not trusting him, for not believing him. She could almost feel his arms as they encircled her and brought her close against him.

With a sigh of expectant pleasure, she walked to the bedroom door, turned the knob, and pulled. The door didn't open. She felt a sudden heaviness in her chest as she tried it again.

The door was locked—from the outside.

Her heart skipped. This couldn't be happening.

Once again she twisted the knob and yanked. Again and again and again.

"No," she whispered. "No. No. No."

From the other side of the door, she heard a deep chuckle.

"Father, what are you doing?"

"Your wedding day has been moved forward, and I'm making sure you're here to enjoy it."

"Father!" She pounded on the door with her fist. "Father, open the door!"

"I can't, Olivia."

She forced herself to be calm. She wouldn't let him hear her panic. "I have never given you reason to believe I won't marry Lord Lambert. Please, open the door. Mother is expecting me to join her for church."

"Your mother isn't going to church today. She has too many things to do in preparation for your wedding next week." His voice grew deeper, closer. "Olivia, if you think you can refuse to marry the viscount when the time comes, do consider what might happen to Mr. Walker. There are so many calamities that could befall him in this city."

She closed her eyes and wilted against the door.

"Just consider it, daughter."

She heard him walk away. "No," she whispered again. She slowly slid down the door until she sat in a puddle of blue skirts on the floor. "You can't do this. You can't."

☙

Remington's gaze searched every pew, but neither Libby nor her mother were in the sanctuary. She may have been absent for a dozen good reasons, but uneasiness nagged at him as he slipped out of the church when the service was over.

As he headed down the sidewalk toward home, he remembered the way Libby had looked last night, the way she watched him as he told her everything. He'd seen a spark of hope in her eyes, a willingness to believe, as she listened. He knew she still cared, whether or not she was willing to admit it. She would contact him after she sorted things through. He had no reason to feel apprehensive. She would send word when she was ready to see him. All he had to do was wait.

Unfortunately his disquiet wouldn't leave him. It grew with every step he took.

Something's wrong . . . Something's wrong . . . The words played through his head, unrelenting, insistent. *Something's wrong . . . Something's wrong . . .*

By the time he reached his brownstone, he'd resolved to see Libby today, and the only way he knew to do that was to pay a visit to Rosegate.

☙

Libby heard the key turn in the lock and rose from the chair near the fireplace. A moment later Sophie entered, carrying a breakfast tray.

"Your father sent something for you to eat, Miss Olivia."

Ignoring the maid, Libby hurried toward the door. If she was especially careful, she might be able to—

"It's no use, Miss Olivia. Your father has someone watching the door. A mean-looking sort, he is, from Mr. Vanderhoff's warehouse."

Libby's heart sank, but she refused to give in to despair. She would find a way out. She had to get to Remington. She had lingered too long in apathy.

"Sophie, you must help me," she said in a low voice as she faced the maid.

The girl shook her head, eyes wide. "I can't. Your father warned me what would happen if I did. I'm a poor girl. I can't afford to be turned out without references."

With a sound of frustration, Libby walked to the window overlooking the street. She wondered if she could climb down the side of the house. If only there were a ledge or a balcony or even a covered porch! But there was nothing but a sheer, three-story drop to the ground.

There must be some way.

A black carriage with its bright green trim pulled to the curb in front of the Vanderhoff mansion. Remington! He'd come for her.

She tried to twist the window latch, but it was stuck. "Open," she demanded as she saw Remington descend from the carriage. As if in obedience, the latch turned.

Before she could call out, hands gripped her upper arms and yanked her backward. "You're to stay away from the window, miss."

She twisted, trying to see the watchdog her father had sent to keep her, but the man shoved her toward her bed. She tripped and fell facedown into the unmade bedding. She heard his chortle as he left the room, closing the door behind him.

"Sophie — " She struggled to her feet but fell silent when she discovered the maid was gone too. She hurried to the door and tried to open it, even though she knew she would find it locked.

The butler led Remington along the dark-paneled hallway toward the back of the house. Libby's father awaited him in a cavernous room, the walls lined with bookshelves, the floor covered with ornate carpeting.

Northrop rose from the chair behind a massive oak desk as Remington entered the study. "Mr. Walker, I didn't know you'd returned to Manhattan."

Liar. "I've been back more than a month now."

Northrop feigned surprise. "You have? Then why haven't you sent round your bill for the rest of your fee? I've been expecting it."

"I haven't sent a bill because I don't want your money." Remington watched Northrop frown, certain the older man took exception to his tone of voice. *That suits me fine.* "I've come to see Libby."

"My daughter's name is Olivia." Northrop sat and motioned to a chair opposite him. "And she isn't receiving visitors."

Remington didn't sit. "She'll see me."

"And why is that, Mr. Walker?"

"Because Libby knows you lied to her. You can't force her to marry the viscount. She's an adult, and she can make her own choice."

"She *has* made her choice. She and the viscount are to be married next week."

"Next week? But the newspaper said — "

"The newspaper made an error."

Remington pressed his knuckles against the desktop. "Then let Libby tell me that for herself."

Northrop leaned back in his chair and eyed Remington as if he were a cockroach on the carpet.

"Unless you're afraid, of course," Remington added softly.

The pendulum in the grandfather clock ticked off the seconds.

At long last, Northrop rose from his chair. "Very well, Mr. Walker. I'll bring my daughter down to see you. And when she has told you of her plans, I shall expect you to leave this house without further trouble. Is that understood?"

"If that's her decision, I'll go."

Libby didn't turn this time when she heard the key in the lock. She remained at the window, staring down at

Remington's carriage, hardly daring to breathe as she waited to see him leave the house.

"Olivia."

She felt an eerie alarm slide up her spine.

"Olivia, Mr. Walker has come to see you."

She turned slowly, fixing her father with a suspicious gaze. "You'll let me see him?"

"Yes. He wants you to tell him that you've made your decision to marry Lord Lambert. He wants you to tell him I'm not forcing the marriage and that it's of your own choice." He moved across the room to stand before her. He placed his index finger beneath her chin. "Before I take you downstairs, I must remind you what might happen to Mr. Walker if you fail to send him away."

You don't frighten me. But that wasn't true. He terrified her. "Have you no heart at all?" She took a step backward, pressing her thighs against the windowsill. "Don't you care for anyone but yourself?"

"Very little, my dear. Now, shall I tell you what to say to your devoted young man?"

"I won't marry Spencer. You cannot make me."

"Ah, but you *will* marry Spencer, and I *can* make you do it. You'll marry the viscount for Mr. Walker's sake . . . and for your mother's. If you don't want either of them to come to harm, you'll do as I say."

"Mama?" She shook her head. "You wouldn't hurt her. She's your wife." But even as she spoke the words, she realized she was wrong.

"You'll go downstairs and tell Mr. Walker that you have made your decision. You are going to marry the viscount. If you don't do as I say, Olivia, your beloved Mr. Walker will find himself in deep water before nightfall. And your mother ..." He left the threat unfinished.

What choice did she have? Remington ... her mother. How else could she protect them from the man who stood before her?

She met her father's eyes with an unwavering gaze of her own. "When I was little, I yearned to win your love. I wondered what was wrong with me. Why you couldn't care for me." She lifted her chin. "But you cannot care. You have sold your soul to the devil and he has poisoned your heart." She stepped around him and headed for the door. "Someday your transgressions will catch up with you, Father, and you'll find the price you must pay for them is more than you possess."

Libby walked swiftly, with her head held high. She didn't look back to see if her father followed.

On the second-floor landing, she paused and glanced down the hall. Was Mama locked in her bedroom too? Was she all right? Libby moved on, descending the stairway to the ground floor. Her mind searched for an idea, some sort of plan, some way to warn Remington of the danger he was in.

God help me, she prayed as she walked down the hall. *Keep him safe.*

Remington heard her footsteps seconds before Libby entered the study. His pulse quickened at the sight of her.

She moved toward him with purposeful strides. "Father says you wanted to see me."

Remington glanced over her shoulder. Northrop stood in the doorway, his arms folded in front of his chest. Glancing back at Libby, Remington said, "I've come to take you away from here."

"I can't go with you." She drew a quick breath. "I'm going to marry Spencer."

He stepped forward, took hold of her arms, and drew her to him. He stared down into wide green eyes. "Is that what you want?"

Her voice grew softer. "It's what I must do, Remington. And you should take the money Father owes you and return to the Blue Springs. Go away from Manhattan. You don't belong here." She drew a breath, then said in a stronger voice, "Tell Sawyer I love him. Tell him not to forget Libby Blue."

Libby Blue. That was it. That's what was different about her. She wore her hair in a braid, like Libby, and her gaze wasn't cool and remote. There was passion in her eyes. He could read love in their depths — and warning too.

His instincts hadn't been wrong. Something was very much amiss here.

"Libby?" he asked softly, testing the name.

"Yes."

In that one word, he heard her confession of love.

"Leave with me."

"I can't."

His fingers squeezed gently. "I understand, Libby. I'll go, since that's what you want me to do." *But I'll be back for you. Don't be afraid. I'll return.*

He could only hope that she understood as he released her and walked out of the study.

Thirty-One

THE VANDERHOFF MANSION LOOMED SHADOWY and large above Seventy-second Street. Thin clouds blew across the three-quarter moon, and shadows and moonlight played a ghostly dance over the stone facing of the house.

Standing across the street, Remington stared at the third-story window, fourth from the left. Sawyer said that was where he'd seen her. Remington hoped it was her bedchamber.

Moving stealthily, he crossed the street and entered through the front gate, then slipped around the side of the house, heading for the servants' entry. At two in the morning, no one was likely to be awake. God willing, Remington could get up to the third floor, wake Libby, and then lead her out. Her absence wouldn't be discovered until she was called to breakfast.

The servants' entrance was locked, but it took Remington only a couple of minutes to open it. He was grateful the door was kept well oiled. It opened and closed without a squeak.

He waited a moment for his eyes to adjust to the darkness before moving into the kitchen, then made his way beyond the pantry and the laundry room, searching for the back staircase. He found it beyond a large, swinging door.

A gas lamp, turned low, cast a dim yellow light on the narrow passageway.

Glancing up, he took a deep breath and began the ascent, praying the boards wouldn't creak beneath his weight. When he reached the third floor, he paused and found his bearings. After a moment, he followed the hallway that would lead him to the chambers facing the street. He stumbled over a chair left in the hall but caught it before it could topple over and send up an alarm. He breathed a sigh of relief as he righted the chair.

He looked up and down the hall, then at the door in front of him. This had to be the room. Libby's room, and the key had been left in the lock. Once more he glanced right, then left. All was silent. With a faint click, he turned the key and opened the door, slipping inside and closing it behind him.

The large four-poster bed was to his left, a giant spiderlike shadow in a room filled with shadows. With blood pounding in his ears, Remington moved toward it, his steps silenced by a thick carpet.

A hand over her mouth brought Libby awake. Terror shot through her, and she tried to pull away, thrashing with her arms, kicking with her legs.

"Libby, it's me."

She quieted, and his hand slid away.

"Come on. We need to get out of here."

She sat up. "Remington." His name slipped from her lips, a verbal caress, filled with hope.

Then he was holding her, kissing her, pushing her hair back from her face. She clung to him, savoring the moment, glad for it, no matter how brief. She breathed in his warm, masculine scent and felt comforted by how familiar it seemed to her.

He lifted his mouth to whisper, "We'd better go. We aren't safe yet."

"Remington, I can't leave." Although she couldn't see him, she sensed his surprise. "Father's threatened to hurt my mother if I don't do what he says. And he's threatened to kill you."

He drew her up from the bed. "We'll take your mother with us. You'll have to show me where her room is."

"But —"

"Don't argue with me, Libby."

Her heart fluttered. "I won't. I'll never argue with you again."

His chuckle was barely audible. "I doubt that." He kissed her. "Now hurry."

She grabbed her dressing gown from the stool at the foot of her bed, slipped her arms into the sleeves, and tied the belt securely around her waist. In the dark, she found a pair of house shoes and put them on. "I'm ready."

He took hold of her hand and led her toward the door. "Where will we find your mother?"

"Second floor, down the hall to the right."

"And where's your father's room?"

"Beyond it one door."

He turned the knob. "Once we're out in the hall, not a word. Understood?"

She nodded, forgetting he couldn't see her in the dark.

He opened the door, and Libby found herself holding her breath. She tightened her grip on Remington's hand as he led her along the hall to the servants' staircase. They descended one floor, and she was thankful for the dim light of the gas lamp, left burning in case one of the Vanderhoffs should ring for something in the night. She was thankful because it afforded her a glimpse of Remington, and she took courage from the sight of him.

When they reached the second-floor landing, he turned to her. "Wait here," he said, his mouth beside her ear.

She shook her head.

He ignored her. "If anything goes wrong, run for it. Get to my place, then send for David Pierce. He's a judge here in the city and an old family friend. Mrs. Blake will know how to get in touch with him. David will be able to help you. You can trust him."

She shook her head again, gripping his hand, refusing to let go.

He kissed her cheek. "It'll be all right, Libby. I won't be long."

Libby felt a sudden *whoosh* of air, then heard a sickening sound, flesh against flesh, bone against bone. Remington jerked free of her hold and went crashing to the floor. She saw his assailant. The brute moved with terrible swiftness, driving his boot into Remington's kidney — once, then again and again.

"Remington!" She tried to intercede but was stayed by the fingers of another closing around her arm.

"I'm afraid your young man is wrong, Olivia." Her father turned her to face him. "He will be a long time in returning."

He stepped toward Remington, lying prone and still on the carpet. "You should have heeded my warning, Walker."

Remington started to speak, but her father's hired thug kicked him again.

Libby groaned, as if she'd been kicked too.

"No one stands in my way, Walker. When they do, I eliminate them, one way or another."

"Like you did . . . my father?"

"Your father?"

Remington tried to sit up but received another kick for his efforts. Gasping for air, he said, "Jefferson . . . Walker."

Libby strained against her father's grasp, to no avail.

"JW . . . Railroad," Remington added.

"JW? Well, I'll be." Her father released a harsh laugh. "You should have learned something from Jefferson. He got in my way too." He shook his head. "And now you'll share his fate." He looked at the man standing over Remington. "Dispose of him, Caswell."

"No, Father! Don't!" She tried to twist free. "Please, I beg you, Father. Don't hurt him anymore. I'll do anything you want. Just don't harm him."

As if he hadn't heard her, her father turned and pulled her with him up the staircase.

Remington regained consciousness in the dank, stinking hold of a ship.

He staggered to his feet, feeling his way in the darkness. Although the floor rocked beneath him, he knew the ship was tied to the pier. He could hear it knocking against the dock as it tugged on its moorings.

How long had he been out? He touched the back of his head, wincing as he felt the lump and dried blood. Next he felt the bruised places on his side and stomach. A cracked rib, maybe, but no permanent damage.

He stood and explored his prison. The exit was barred, the hold windowless. There was no way out. No way he could get to Libby. No way he could help her. No way he could help himself.

He sank to the floor, holding his head in his hands, help-lessness flooding through him. "God, I can't do it without You. Father, my life — and Libby's — are in Your hands."

The ship creaked and moaned.

Disjointed thoughts drifted through Remington's mind. He thought of Libby, of Sawyer, of his boyhood home, of his father. He thought of the years he'd lost to his quest for revenge. He thought of the faith he'd lost, then found again. He'd wasted so much of his life in hate and bitterness. Was this to be where it ended?

"You should have learned something from Jefferson. He got in my way too. And now you'll share his fate."

As Northrop's words echoed in Remington's memory, he felt a strange calm overtake him. He couldn't have explained it, but somehow he knew in his spirit that his father hadn't taken his own life. Jefferson Walker hadn't turned his back on his God or on his son. No matter how deeply he had despaired, he wouldn't have committed suicide.

Remington wondered if this certainty in his heart was God's gift to him before he died. If so —

Something crashed to the deck overhead. The sound was followed by footsteps, then the creak of a door as it opened. Remington raised an arm against the light spilling into the hold.

"'Tis poor company you're keeping, Mr. Walker. Might you be in need of assistance?"

"O'Reilly?"

"Aye. So it is."

Remington got to his feet. "What are you doing here?"

"'Tis a strange story, best saved 'til we're off this boat, I'm thinkin'."

God sent you, O'Reilly. Whether you know it or not. Thank You, Lord.

Remington moved as quickly as his bruised body allowed. Once on deck, he saw Caswell being led away by a police officer.

O'Reilly chuckled. "He'll not be tellin' Mr. Vanderhoff what happened here today. Me friend, Officer O'Hara, will be seein' to that. I'm thinkin' that will help you get to the wee lass with less trouble."

"I don't understand." Remington rubbed the sore spot on his head. "This isn't your fight, O'Reilly."

The Irishman shook his head as he guided Remington to a waiting coach. "'Tis sorry I am for the part I played in Miss Vanderhoff's troubles. I saw the way it was when we come back from Idaho, and me heart nearly broke for her. Count this as me way of askin' your forgiveness. Hers too. This and me offer to help you get the wee lass away from her father." He opened the coach door for Remington. "Sure and I'm thinkin' we've got little to fight Vanderhoff with but our wits. We'd best be makin' plans. Her wedding's not long off."

Thirty-Two

LIBBY WOULD MARRY THE VISCOUNT, but she would not cower before her father. Not ever again. If there had been only herself to think about, she would have refused to do his bidding. If he killed her, so be it. After all, Remington was dead, so her own life mattered little now. But in order to protect her mother, she would go through with this sham of a marriage.

Every day the dressmaker came to Rosegate, to Libby's room, for the fittings of her wedding gown. Mrs. Davenport never let on if she thought the bride's behavior odd. She chattered about the Parisian gown made of ivory satin, draped with Brussels lace, and trimmed with orange blossoms. She said how wonderful it was that Libby would marry an English lord. "Never has Manhattan seen such a beautiful bride as you will be, Miss Vanderhoff. You'll take England by storm. Mark my words."

But Libby cared nothing about England, nothing about her wedding — except that to marry Spencer meant protecting her mother. And it meant putting an ocean between her and her father, too. The one thing it could not do was separate her from her memories of Remington. Her father could not succeed in doing that.

In those moments when sorrow threatened to overwhelm her, she clung to her belief in God's love and ultimate goodness. Evil might swirl around her on this earth, but she wouldn't let go of her faith. She wouldn't allow herself to sink into apathetic lethargy. Not again.

Her wedding day arrived with gray skies and cold October winds. At dawn, Libby watched from her bedchamber window as the sky turned from onyx to pewter. Leaves tumbled from tree limbs, rolling along the street, slipping beneath the wheels of delivery wagons, where they were crushed into dust. Extra servants hired for the wedding festivities leaned into the wind and held on to their hats as they made their way toward the rear entrance of the Vanderhoff house.

She pressed her forehead against the cool glass, wishing for a moment that she could open the window and let the wind blow her away like the autumn leaves.

Father God, keep me strong. If it be Your will, stop this wedding. Help me find another way to protect my mother. Your will be done, Lord.

Remington kept his cap pulled low and his head bent forward as he carted chairs into the Vanderhoff ballroom, ever watchful for a chance to slip away from the other temporary help and make his way up the stairs. And he prayed. Prayed harder than he'd ever prayed in his life.

Show me the way, Lord. Show me the way.

Wedding guests had begun to arrive before Remington found the opportunity he'd prayed for. In an unprecedented moment when no one else was near, he slipped away from the other workers and climbed the back staircase to the third floor.

Just as he reached the top of the stairs, the door to Libby's room opened and a maid stepped into the hall. Remington watched until she walked down the hall and disappeared into another room, then strode toward his destination.

The door wasn't locked. He opened it and stepped inside.

His gaze found Libby at once. She stood before the cheval glass, clad in a wedding gown. Two women fussed about her, an older matron fastening the pearl buttons up the back of the gown — the other, a young maid about Libby's age, kneeling on the floor, doing something to the hem.

The older woman turned her head when she heard the door click shut. She let out a tiny gasp of surprise when she saw Remington. "What are you doing here, sir?"

He ignored her as he started forward.

The woman stepped into his path. "Get out of here at once, or I shall be forced to — "

"Libby."

He saw her stiffen, then she turned around. Color drained from her face. Her lips moved, but no sound came out.

"Jeanette, send for Mr. Vanderhoff," the older woman ordered. "Quickly. Tell him — "

"No." Libby stopped the seamstress with a hand on her arm. "No, please. It's all right, Mrs. Davenport." She came toward him, stepping around Mrs. Davenport, who hadn't budged an inch. "You're here."

"I'm here. I've come to take you home."

"I thought you were dead."

"No. I'm alive."

"You're alive." She reached up, touching his face with her fingertips. Her eyes were wide, unblinking, as if she were afraid he might disappear. "You really are alive."

He grabbed one of her hands, turned it, and brought it to his lips, kissing her palm. "Very much so."

"Thank God. Oh, thank God."

"Yes, it's the Lord we have to thank."

"Father said—"

"He lied. Are you ready to marry me and return to the Blue Springs? Sawyer's waiting for us."

"I'm ready." She almost smiled. "I've been ready to marry you for quite some time."

Mrs. Davenport gasped.

Remington reached into his pocket and withdrew the bank draft he'd brought with him. "This is to leave for your father." He handed it to Libby.

Libby stared at the draft. It was made out to Northrop Vanderhoff.

"That's every penny he's paid me. I thought we should leave it for him."

Her vision blurred with unshed tears. "You don't have to give this back."

"I don't want his money, Libby. I want only his daughter. Let's get your mother and go home."

Home. We're going home . . .

"You'll need to change out of that wedding gown," Remington said, a hint of humor in his voice, "or we'll never slip out this house unnoticed."

She turned, prepared to tell Mrs. Davenport to unfasten the buttons up the back of the gown. But then she stopped. "No, Remington. We can't go that way."

"What do you mean? I've got help waiting —"

"We can't sneak away. I can't keep running from him." She stared into his beloved eyes, beseeching him to understand. "I've run away too often in the past. I can't run again. We've got to face him together, Remington. If we don't, he'll have won."

Thirty-Three

NORTHROP BECAME AWARE OF A hush rippling across the crowd of guests. He looked up to find his daughter standing in the ballroom doorway. She looked spectacular in her wedding gown, every inch a countess. But with her, dressed like one of the servants, stood Remington Walker, holding her arm with fierce protectiveness.

"Who is that with Olivia?" someone whispered.

Someone else answered, "That's Remington Walker. Why's he dressed like that?"

Other voices murmured throughout the room.

Then Northrop saw Anna standing behind their daughter. His wife wore a yellow silk gown. Yellow, the color he'd forbidden her to wear because he knew it was her favorite.

Northrop realized in that instant that his daughter would never be a countess.

❧

Unafraid, Libby stared at her father. She felt free, like an eagle soaring high above the rugged Idaho mountains.

Stand fast therefore in the liberty wherewith Christ hath made us free, and be not entangled again with the yoke of bondage.

She and Remington, followed by her mother, moved through the throng of guests who parted like water before a ship's bow. She heard their whispers but ignored them. She didn't care what was said or by whom. She had come to say good-bye to her father — and to Olivia Vanderhoff.

Northrop glared as they approached. She saw his frustration in the set of his mouth, knew he controlled a blinding rage that would erupt later. Pity the person who was nearby when it happened.

Stopping a few feet away, she held out the bank draft Remington had given her upstairs. "We've come to give you this, Father."

His frown deepened as he reached to take the draft.

"And to say good-bye. I'm not going to marry the viscount." As a collective gasp arose behind her, she shifted her gaze to her shocked fiancé. "I'm sorry, Spencer. I cannot marry you when I love someone else." Once more she looked at her father. "I won't be sold like some product in your warehouse, and I won't be held prisoner in my room. I'm going to walk out that door, free to do as God leads me. I'm going to marry Remington, and then I'm returning to our ranch in Idaho."

The buzz of voices increased.

"Everything you paid to search for me is there. You can't keep us apart, no matter what lies you tell, no matter what else you do."

In a voice that carried across the ballroom, Remington said, "And you shouldn't be surprised to know Mrs. Vanderhoff is coming with us when we go."

Northrop's face blazed red with fury. "Anna, you'll never get a divorce as long as — "

"I'm not asking for one. I will choose God's edicts over yours." Anna turned toward the shocked guests. "I'm sorry, everyone, but there will be no wedding in this house today. Now, please excuse me. I must pack a few things. I'm leaving New York." She smiled at her daughter. "I'm going to Idaho with Libby and her new husband. Believe it or not, I'm going to raise sheep instead of roses."

Epilogue

July 1894
Blue Springs Ranch, Idaho

Roses were in full bloom in Anna's garden, a kaleido-scope of color at the back of the Blue Springs Ranch house. From the kitchen window, Libby Walker watched as her mother, ever the gentlewoman, settled her skirts around her on the wooden bench. After a moment's hesitation, Alistair McGregor sat beside her.

"Ye'll know why I've come, Anna," the Scotsman said, just loud enough for Libby to hear him.

"My love, who're you spying on?"

She jumped at the sound of Remington's voice. Then, with a finger to her lips, she motioned her husband to join her at the window. "McGregor's finally going to do it."

"Propose?"

She nodded.

Remington put an arm around Libby's shoulders, say-ing softly, "This should be good."

Libby elbowed him in the ribs.

"Anna," McGregor continued, unaware that he had an audience other than the woman beside him, "yer husband's been dead more than two years now, and ye cannot be ignorant of what I feel for ye. I've a house for ye now and enough land for ye to bury us in roses, if that would please ye. So I've come t'ask ye t'be my bride."

Say yes, Mama. You love him, too. Say yes.

Before she could hear her mother's reply, Remington drew her away from the window. "Rem—" she started to protest.

"They deserve their privacy, love. Besides, it sounds to me like our son is awake and demanding to be fed."

Libby heard twelve-week-old Jeff's mewling coming from the children's bedroom. A tingle of sheer joy shot through her. God had blessed her beyond her wildest dreams. A husband who adored her and two beautiful, healthy children— Amanda Ann Walker, an adorable but headstrong three-year-old; and Jefferson O'Reilly Walker, a sweet-natured baby who rarely fussed.

It was difficult to believe more than four years had passed since Remington walked through a grove of trees under the cover of night and changed her life forever.

The front door slammed. "Ma?"

"In the kitchen," Libby answered, keeping her voice low, hoping not to bother the lovebirds in the backyard. *I hope you said yes, Mama.*

Sawyer entered the room. One look at Libby and Remington and he asked, "What's going on?" At fourteen, their adopted son was no longer a boy. Tall and lanky, his voice had changed to the deep timbre of a man, and he'd even started to shave, though he only needed to use the razor once or twice a week at most.

Remington jerked his head toward the window. "McGregor's asked your grandmother to marry him."

"Well, I'll be. It's about time." Sawyer grabbed a cookie off the plate on the table and took a bite.

"Don't fill up on those," Libby scolded. "It will be suppertime before you know it."

Jeff's cries became more insistent, but he was drowned out by his sister's "Mama!"

Remington kissed Libby's cheek. "Sounds like Amanda Ann's up from her nap."

Thank You, Father. Thank You for all these blessings. What mercy and grace You have showered upon me, even when my faith was too small.

She recalled the words of a poem she'd read last night:

If I have freedom in my love,
*   And in my soul am free,*
Angels alone that soar above
*   Enjoy such liberty.*

Libby smiled at the simple truth, feeling as if the poet had written those words for her alone. Only when she'd given herself in love—to God's love first, then to Remington's—had she become truly free. Only when she'd risked her heart had she found the ability to soar like the angels.

"Mama!"

"I'm coming, Amanda Ann," she called, then looked up into her husband's eyes, saying softly, "I love you, Remington. Thank you for making my heart soar."

Dear Lady

Robin Lee Hatcher

In the big-sky country of Montana, the past doesn't always stay buried. Circumstances have a way of forcing secrets into the open, sometimes bringing hearts together in unlikely ways, and sometimes tearing them apart.

Dear Lady is Book One in the Coming to America series about women who come to America to start new lives. Set in the late 1800s and early 1900s, these novels by bestselling author Robin Lee Hatcher craft intense chemistry and conflict between the characters, lit by a glowing faith and humanity that will win your heart. Look for other books in the series at your favorite Christian bookstore.

Softcover: 978-0-310-23083-0

Patterns of Love

Robin Lee Hatcher

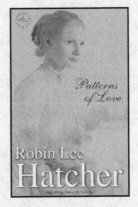

In rural Iowa, life is both the planter and uprooter of dreams. As love, long delayed, springs to life in the heart of a young Swedish immigrant, one man struggles with his withered ambitions— and new blessings that could take their place if he would but allow them room.

Patterns of Love is Book Two in the Coming to America series.

Softcover: 978-0-310-23105-9

In His Arms

Robin Lee Hatcher

Idaho: mountainous, rugged. Men go there to find their fortunes in the silver mines—and lose their pasts. But as Mary Malone discovers, sometimes the past is not so easily shaken. It will take a good man's strong, persistent love to penetrate the young immigrant's defenses and disarm the secret that makes a hostage of her heart.

In His Arms is Book Three in the Coming to America series.

Softcover: 978-0-310-23120-2

Promised to Me

Robin Lee Hatcher

In Idaho, the land is good but life is hard for a German émigré whose dreams have turned to dust. Love found and lost can shatter a man's faith. But it is about to strengthen that of the woman to whom he turns—and in the drought of summer, a withered promise springs to life.

Promised to Me is Book Four in the Coming to America series.

Softcover: 978-0-310-23555-2

Share Your Thoughts

With the Author: Your comments will be forwarded to
the author when you send them to *zauthor@zondervan.com*.

With Zondervan: Submit your review of this book
by writing to *zreview@zondervan.com*.

Free Online Resources at
www.zondervan.com/hello

 Zondervan AuthorTracker: Be notified whenever your favorite authors publish new books, go on tour, or post an update about what's happening in their lives.

 Daily Bible Verses and Devotions: Enrich your life with daily Bible verses or devotions that help you start every morning focused on God.

 Free Email Publications: Sign up for newsletters on fiction, Christian living, church ministry, parenting, and more.

 Zondervan Bible Search: Find and compare Bible passages in a variety of translations at www.zondervanbiblesearch.com.

 Other Benefits: Register yourself to receive online benefits like coupons and special offers, or to participate in research.